THE NINTH URBAN FARM FRESH ROMANCE

Lavished with Lavender

VALERIE COMER

GreenWords Media

ACKNOWLEDGMENTS

This novel was written in March and April, 2020, during the time the coronavirus pandemic stomped on our world with steel-spiked boots. Like many others, I became paralyzed with anxiety, watching too much online news and too many opinion pieces. I couldn't bear the thought of writing a "frivolous" romance novel as borders closed, workers were laid off in droves, and hospitals filled with sick. As people died.

But then God reminded me of 1 Peter 5:7, which reads, 'Cast all your anxiety on him because he cares for you.' And Philippians 4:6-7, which says, 'Do not be anxious about anything, but in everything by prayer and supplication with thanksgiving let your requests be made known to God.'

And God soothed my soul. He reminded me that I'd already chosen the title and written several chapters where themes of releasing stress and anxiety to Jesus had begun to peek through. God was preparing my thoughts to rest on Him in the midst of a bigger trial than I could ever have imagined.

As Marietta's family gathered for her eightieth birthday, I wanted to tell all of them they should be self-isolating! That they needed to allow six feet between everyone. I realized that if I allowed the pandemic into Bridgeview, the story of a chef and a nurse would completely veer into left field, just as all our lives did when the globe shut down in mid-March. Will I ever write stories set in the time of COVID-19? Impossible to know, but it won't be in the Urban Farm Fresh Romance series!

Thanks to Elizabeth Maddrey, first reader, idea-bouncer and excellent author in your own right. Thank you for providing sanity, humor, and kicks in the pants as needed!

Also thank you to beta readers Gretchen, Joy, Paula, and Joelle. Your comments helped tighten and improve this story!

Thanks to some of my newsletter subscribers who gave me hoarding ideas I could use in this story: Diane, Jan, Kimberly, Kitty, Margaret, Marilene, and Erin. I hope you enjoyed your early copies :)

A big thank you to my fabulous editor, Nicole, who sees beyond words, punctuation, and sentence structure to the heart of the story.

I'm also grateful for the Christian Indie Authors Facebook group and my sister bloggers at Inspy Romance. These folks make a difference in my life every single day. I'm thrilled to walk beside them as we tell stories for Jesus!

Thank you to my Facebook friends, followers, street team, and reader group members for prayers, encouragement, and great fellowship.

Thanks to my husband, Jim, for research trips to Spokane and talking through scenarios as needed — to say nothing of everyday love and support — and to my kids and grandgirls for cheering me on and embracing the idiosyncrasies of having an author for a mom and grandmother.

All my love and gratitude goes to Jesus, the One who invited me to experience His unending and passionate love and walks beside me every day. My prayer is that you see His love anew through the pages of this story.

Valerie Comer Bibliography

Urban Farm Fresh Romance

0. Promise of Peppermint (ebook only)
1. Secrets of Sunbeams
2. Butterflies on Breezes
3. Memories of Mist
4. Wishes on Wildflowers
5. Flavors of Forever
6. Raindrops on Radishes
7. Dancing at Daybreak
8. Glimpses of Gossamer
9. Lavished with Lavender

Christmas in Montana Romance

1. More Than a Tiara
2. Other Than a Halo
3. Better Than a Crown

Farm Fresh Romance

1. Raspberries and Vinegar
2. Wild Mint Tea
3. Sweetened with Honey
4. Dandelions for Dinner
5. Plum Upside Down
6. Berry on Top

Saddle Springs Romance
(Montana Ranches Christian Romance)

1. The Cowboy's Christmas Reunion
2. The Cowboy's Mixed-Up Matchmaker
3. The Cowboy's Romantic Dreamer
4. The Cowboy's Convenient Marriage
5. The Cowboy's Belated Discovery
6. The Cowboy's Reluctant Bride

Garden Grown Romance
(Arcadia Valley Romance)

1. Sown in Love (ebook only)
2. Sprouts of Love
3. Rooted in Love
4. Harvest of Love

Riverbend Romance Novellas

1. Secretly Yours
2. Pinky Promise
3. Sweet Serenade
4. Team Bride
5. Merry Kisses

valeriecomer.com/books

1

Sitting in her car at the curb was not going to get Kenna Johnson this position. She took a deep breath and stared at the white stucco house. Four women waited inside to see if she'd pass muster as an acceptable caregiver for their mother-in-law's convalescence.

Marietta Santoro. The world's bossiest busybody.

Kenna's late husband's derisive voice echoed in her head. But then, Maurice Hamelin never had anything good to say about anyone, his wife included. She'd stuck with him, though, a man thirty years her senior. If she could handle Maurice, she could handle Marietta.

And she needed this job.

Show time.

She breathed a quick prayer to a God she didn't really know, slid out of her car, and strode up the walk. Before she could reach for the doorbell, the door swung open, and a woman of about sixty offered a bright smile.

"Hi. You must be Makenna? I'm Genevera Santoro. Come on in."

Kenna gave the woman's hand a firm shake. "Yes, that's me. Pleased to meet you."

Genevera introduced her cohorts: Grace, Winnie, and Betta. Together, they made up the local contingent of the old lady's daughters-in-law.

Kenna smiled and nodded at each of them in turn before taking in the living room packed with the evidence of a full life. Furniture, knickknacks, and two walls crammed with ornately framed photos of graduations and weddings and babies.

Maurice had rejected her notion of hanging anything, even an old painting from the thrift store. Certainly not portraits of his sons, since he'd despised them. The feeling had been mutual.

"Please, have a seat." Genevera motioned toward a club chair. "Can I get you a coffee?"

"No, thank you." This wasn't a social call. Kenna perched on the edge of the seat and launched into her spiel. "I achieved my Bachelor of Nursing at Gonzaga U ten years ago and worked at the nursing home for several years before taking time away to nurse my late husband through his final days. Since then, I've picked up shifts at Deaconess Hospital, but nothing permanent full-time, so I applied with the home-care agency."

"Your references are impeccable," Winnie assured her. "And the agency highly recommended you."

They'd better have.

"Tell us a bit about yourself." Grace leaned forward. "What are your hobbies?"

Kenna blinked. Hobbies? Who had time for anything like that? "I prefer to work."

Genevera smiled. "You can't work all the time, though. Do you enjoy reading? Knitting? Gardening?"

Right, the Bridgeview area of Spokane was particularly big on gardening. She'd circled the block earlier and caught glimpses of Marietta's lush backyard through the tall fence. She'd probably be expected to help with the old lady's yard. Marietta sure wouldn't be doing much over the next few months, not with a cracked pelvis, broken ribs, and her arm in a cast after a nasty fall a couple of weeks ago.

"Sure, I like gardening." Kenna liked whatever would get her this position. Anything to get away from the head nurse on her ward, who seemed to have it in for her. As if Kenna could help attracting crude remarks from little old men. Maurice had been adept at them, too.

"And you're okay with moving in for a few months? From what the doctor at the rehab center said, Mamma will need assistance until at least Thanksgiving."

"Yes, I'm fine with that. I can sublet my apartment."

"It entails more than nursing." Winnie eyed her. "Cooking, cleaning, running the household…"

"No problem." She might not be the most inventive cook, but she could get meals on the table. It would work out. And cleaning? That filled any spare time. She already itched to dust the baseboards and straighten a crooked frame. "Which is your mother-in-law's favorite chair? Will she be able to access it from her wheelchair?"

Winnie pointed to a wide armchair with low arms. "She loves to sit there where she can watch the street. She usually has a knitting project on the go, but I guess she won't be doing that for a while. Not with her arm in a cast."

"You'll need to remove one of the side tables by her

chair." Kenna glanced around the living room. "The space is way too crowded for a wheelchair."

"Yes, the agency did a home study." Genevera nodded. "We have a list of requirements from a ramp to the front door to grab bars in her bathroom to... well, the list is long."

"We have a family work day planned," put in Grace.

"Good. What day do they expect to discharge her?" As in, what would Kenna's start date be?

"Wednesday afternoon, if we're ready. It will be a push for us, but they need the rehab bed for someone else."

"Does that work for you?" asked Winnie. "The agency said they could provide a wheelchair-accessible van to bring her home."

Today was Friday. Kenna nodded. "Wednesday is fine. I can pick her up from the unit and bring her here. I'd prefer to move in the day before if at all possible. At least, if I've met with your approval, and you'd like to hire me?" She held her breath a moment, watching the women glance at each other. *Please, please, please.*

"May I show you around the house?" asked Betta. She'd been rather quiet through the whole interview.

"Sure." That would give the others time to consult behind her back. Whatever. Kenna rose and followed Betta into a large kitchen lined with granite countertops. "This is nice." More than nice. It was a dream kitchen for a serious cook, probably four or five times the size of the one in Kenna's apartment. But then, she normally made do with quick, basic meals.

"Mamma loves to cook." Betta pointed out the doors to a patio where grapes dangled from the roof supports. Beyond it lay a yard lined with raised beds filled with tomato plants and others Kenna didn't recognize. "And she loves her fresh ingredients. Don't worry, her grandchildren will take care of most of this garden."

Whew. The sound of a gate clicking caught her attention, and a man in denim shorts and a gray T-shirt rounded the corner of the house.

"There's Tony now. Have you met him before?"

Kenna shook her head, but she wasn't sure. All the Santoro guys looked a lot alike with their wiry builds, dark curly hair, and striking blue eyes.

"Tony lives in the basement right now. He's very busy with his new restaurant. You may have noticed Antonio's just a few blocks away?"

Kenna blinked. She'd driven by at times over the winter and watched the transformation of a nondescript building to an inviting Mediterranean-style villa. She should have guessed it was a Santoro enterprise. "Yes, I've seen it."

"Don't worry. My nephew isn't here much. He won't be in your way."

Just the thought of someone else coming and going at odd hours was enough to be in Kenna's way.

Betta opened the patio door and leaned out. "Tony! I'd like you to meet one of the applicants for nursing Nonna."

His head came up, and he met her gaze with assessing eyes. "Hi, there." He came inside the back door. "I'm Tony. And you are...?"

"Makenna Johnson," supplied Betta.

His eyebrows rose. "Johnson? That's not what I heard."

Kenna straightened her shoulders and stared back. "I go by Kenna Johnson again." There was no keeping Maurice a secret, not when she'd lived less than a mile from here for six years as his wife. Besides, Grace Santoro, at least, knew who she was. "It's the name on my nursing diploma."

Betta's gaze zipped between them. "Is there a problem, Tony?"

"I don't know. Is there a problem... Ms. Johnson?"

WHAT HAD COME OVER HIM? His words sounded challenging. Mean, even. So not like him.

Tony Santoro had known his aunts were hiring a nurse for Nonna. His cousin Jasmine had told him her late father-in-law's fourth and final wife was on the short list of prospects. She'd even mentioned that Makenna was quite a lot younger than Maurice had been. He'd still somehow envisioned a plump, middle-aged woman with a ready smile — someone comfortable — not a blond bombshell with sharp edges on her attitude.

Back when he and his sister had been kids, Gina had been obsessed with her fashion doll collection. This nurse jogged his memory with her long wavy hair, tanned skin, and hourglass figure. Probably just as airheaded.

Her chin came up and steely gray eyes bored into his. "There is no problem, Mr. Santoro."

"Tony?" Aunt Betta was all but wringing her hands. "What's going on?"

He hadn't reacted this strongly to anyone in years, negatively or positively. And this was definitely negative. How could someone who looked so... perfect... take good care of his beloved grandmother? How many hours did she spend on those fingernails, anyway?

Tony turned away. "I need to pick the tomatoes before I head down to the restaurant. We're featuring Caprese tonight."

"Tony?" asked Aunt Betta again.

"He may have known me as Makenna Hamelin." The nurse's words clipped out. "My resume mentions my time as Maurice Hamelin's nurse through his final days." She took a deep breath. "Your sister-in-law Grace knew I was married to him."

Tony couldn't resist one last poke. "What did he die of, Ms. Johnson?"

"Cirrhosis of the liver, Mr. Santoro. He was a heavy drinker, and it caught up to him." She leaned a little closer, her heels putting her eyes nearly on level with his. "If you think I married him for his money or helped him to his death, you accuse me unjustly."

"From what I heard, he had no money."

"Exactly."

"So why did you marry a man old enough to be your father?"

He'd thought her gaze direct and steely before, but it sharpened considerably. "I don't see it as any of your business, Mr. Santoro."

"You're right. Pardon me, please." Ugh. He'd been rude. He needed out of Nonna's breakfast room. Tony reached for the knob on the patio door behind him.

Kenna turned to Aunt Betta. "The information truly didn't seem to be necessary on a professional document. My marital history has no bearing on whether or not I'm a good nurse."

Aunt Grace strode around the table, hooked her hand around Tony's arm, and guided him outside. The door clicked shut behind them.

Tony felt like a little kid who'd been caught misbehaving

as he looked down into his aunt's eyes. "I'm sorry. I shouldn't have—"

"We need a nurse for your nonna, Tony."

He braced himself. "I know." If only he could do it himself, but it wasn't possible. He knew that.

"And, frankly, she's the best of the lot who applied. I knew she'd been Maurice's wife. If anything, I applaud her for staying with him until the end. The man cannot have been easy to live with."

That was a different spin, but it made sense. Tony nodded.

"However, we'll keep looking if there's going to be a problem between you and her. There was another woman closer to my age who applied, but she had back surgery three years ago, and I'm worried she might not be strong enough to assist Nonna. Plus, she doesn't wish to move in."

Nonna wasn't a tiny woman. Sturdy might be the most polite way to put it.

"So we need to know if it's a problem. Because we need the best possible person for your nonna, but you do live here, too."

Tony took a deep breath and let it out slowly. "I'm really not here very much. The restaurant takes up so much of my time."

Aunt Grace nodded. Waited.

He shoved his hands through his hair. "Do what's best for Nonna. It's just for a few months. I'll stay out of Makenna's way."

"What about Kenna struck you negatively?"

It seemed petty to say because of her looks. There was only so much a person could do about the... assets... God had given them. Although it looked to him like Makenna —

Kenna — was both aware of her features and knew how to use them to her best advantage.

"She reminds me of someone." A fashion doll, but Aunt Grace didn't need to know that. Besides, would a real airhead have a nursing degree? Unlikely. "It's not her fault. If you truly believe she's the best person for Nonna, go ahead."

Aunt Grace squeezed his arm. "Thank you. I'll let you know what we decide, but we are leaning toward offering her the position. Either way, we'll have a family workday on Wednesday to arrange things for a wheelchair and a hospital-style bed for Nonna. I hope you'll be able to spare a few hours to help out, but if not, we understand."

No doubt all his cousins would take the day off work and show up en force, but could Tony do the same? Nope. Not without closing Antonio's and giving his staff the night off. "I can pitch in for a couple of hours in the morning. Or I can fix lunch for the work crew if that's more help." Nonna's kitchen was a pleasure to cook in.

"Lunch would be great. Thank you." Aunt Grace turned toward the door then glanced back at him. "You won't regret having Kenna around, Tony. It will be a relief for all of us, including you, to have someone caring for Nonna."

He looked through the glass door to see Makenna and the aunts watching him and Aunt Grace. Makenna's perfect eyebrows rose as she stared coolly at him.

Tony stifled a snort. Relief to have her around? Not hardly.

$\mathcal{K}$enna braced herself as Tony walked away without a backward glance, and Grace reentered the kitchen. Men. They either fell all over themselves for her attention or hated her on sight. It was easier to deal with the haters.

The four women exchanged looks and tiny nods she was certain she wasn't supposed to notice. She hadn't survived six years with Maurice without keeping a close watch on nuances. That man's temper flipped with little warning.

Grace extended her hand, drawing Kenna's eye. "We'd like to offer you the position."

Kenna blinked then allowed a smile to cross her face. "Thank you. I know you won't regret it." *Take that, Mr. Hot Shot Chef.* "If I'm to live in, may I see my quarters?"

"Absolutely. There are two bedrooms on this level aside from the master suite." Grace beckoned, and Kenna followed her down the hallway. "This one is set up as a guest room already. It's where Tony's parents stay when they visit from Galena Landing in Idaho, but they can stay with Ray and me when they come for family events this fall."

Kenna peered into the room stuffed with mismatched furniture, including a queen bed covered with a handmade quilt. "And the other one? I'd hate to take their room."

"Well, the other one is Mamma's sewing room." Grace opened the door. "There is a twin bed, though."

The sight of shelving units overflowing with fabrics and craft supplies made Kenna flinch. Open boxes sat on the narrow bed, revealing ribbons, lace, and other notions. This room was an absolute no-go unless it were gutted, and she couldn't be that cruel to her client.

"I do hate to take up the only guest room, but this space isn't an option."

Grace nodded thoughtfully. "I understand. Mamma is a bit of a packrat."

Understatement of the century.

"We've tried to encourage her to sort through some of this, but she's resisted. Plus, we're all busy with work and our own families. It just hasn't become a priority."

Oh, boy. "So, this bedroom." Kenna turned back to the guest space. "Are the drawers and closet stuffed as well? I'm not sure where I'd put my things."

Grace crossed to the closet and opened the bifold doors. Coats. Dresses. Suits. Stacks of pillows and baskets of shoes. Pursing her lips, she tugged open one of the drawers. Full of linens. The next one was full of black socks.

Seriously? Socks? Kenna had no words.

"I'm sorry. These must have been my father-in-law's. I didn't realize she hadn't gotten rid of his things."

When had the man passed away? Mrs. Santoro had been

widowed before Kenna had moved to this part of the city eight years ago.

Grace straightened her shoulders. "I promise we'll completely clear out this room for you before Tuesday. What pieces of furniture would you like to use? We'll remove the rest."

"The bed will be useful. The nightstand. The dresser with the mirror." Mentally, Kenna cleared the space and felt the bands around her skull loosen. "I think that will be enough."

"Consider it done."

"Thank you." She only hoped the older woman could — and would — follow through. "My primary focus, of course, will be Mrs. Santoro's health and wellbeing. I can care for the house. I'm not the world's best cook, but I'll manage."

"Tony has been cooking for his grandmother some. Bringing her meals from the restaurant or filling her fridge with leftovers."

"How kind of him, but that won't be necessary any longer. From what you've said, meals are part of my duties." The less she saw of that particular man, the better. He didn't trust her. That street went both ways. She didn't trust him, either. Not after the measuring look and the disdain in his eyes.

None of which mattered. She'd been married once, and she was never going there again. All she needed to get her foot in the door with a full-time nursing job was a good recommendation from the Santoros. Then she'd be set for life. She was no stranger to being alone. It was a vast improvement over depending on someone else.

"That table of four who stayed so long last night? Turns out they were culinary reviewers with a popular Instagram feed." Tony's maître d' stood in the kitchen doorway, tablet in hand.

Tony looked up from showing his new assistant how to butterfly a chicken breast. "Oh? How'd we do?"

Eduardo grinned. "Flying colors, chef."

Whew. "Send me the link, would you? I'd like to see it."

"You got it, chef." He tapped a few times. "Sent."

"Thanks." Tony watched Oriana bite hard on her bottom lip as she gingerly sliced at the chicken. At this rate, it would take her five minutes to do each one. Would she gain confidence and speed up, or should he look through the stack of resumes for someone else? But she'd been the best of the lot last week. There couldn't be that many new applications since then.

"Oh!" Oriana's knife angled downward and she looked up at Tony, eyes wide with apprehension.

He'd never thought of himself as a perfectionist before opening Antonio's. Sure, as a chef, he'd always prided himself in doing his best, but it was different being completely in charge. In his uncle's Twin Falls kitchen, Tony would have simply reported the problem, and Uncle Leo would have dealt with the staff.

Here, it was all on Tony. He'd fired his last assistant, a middle-aged man who hadn't taken kindly to the young upstart's decisions. Ageism wasn't something Tony had considered when planning his own restaurant, but it was real. Not only that, but he'd been open four months now and was still shaking down his staff. He'd gone through more servers than he could count, and he'd soon be looking again when the college year began.

Interviewing and training staff should not be taking up as much of his time as it did.

Tony held out his hand for the knife, and Oriana handed it over. He examined the chicken breast and shook his head before whacking it into chunks and scraping it aside. He'd adapt tonight's menu if there were too many more like this. "Too uneven. Try again."

"Okay." She looked between the pile of meat and him.

He got the message. "I'll check on you in a bit."

Oriana nodded and reached for the next.

Tony couldn't watch. He pivoted into his office and checked for Eduardo's email on his phone. The link took him to a carousel of images of last night's dining experience, including the special, swordfish with porcini risotto. He remembered plating this order.

Relief washed over him as he closed his eyes. Thankfully this group had enjoyed amazing food, exemplary service, and great wine… unlike the less enthralled couple from the previous week with their mediocre review. #room2improve was not a hashtag he wanted to ever see again.

Lord? Please give me wisdom.

That was his constant prayer these days. He'd known there was more to opening his own restaurant than cooking. He just hadn't realized how much of his time that would take. Uncle Leo made it look easy at Italiana in Twin Falls, but he'd been in business for over thirty years. The growing pains had long since been dealt with.

Back at it. Tony had no time for self-indulgent whining. They'd be opening in half an hour, and there was plenty of prep still to go.

TONY CLOSED Nonna's gate behind him and inhaled the fragrance of an August garden at rest. Tomatoes. Lavender. Squash. The mingled scents soothed him and triggered the relaxation process. The motion sensor activated the light by the basement door, and he tapped the code to unlock it.

The little suite took up less than half the total floor-space and had been filled with castoff furniture from upstairs when he moved in. That was fine. He didn't have any of his own. He'd split rent on an apartment with Levi Esteban in Seattle during their culinary school years, and he'd shared a house with several guys in Arcadia Valley, a small town near Twin Falls, for the past few years. Someday he'd have his own place, but he was in no hurry. Right now, his life was consumed by Antonio's.

But something was out of place. The bookcase filled with his favorite paperbacks had been shifted down the wall and an ornate highboy had been wedged in beside it.

Tony crossed over and pulled open a drawer. Full of junk. He should have known. He looked in his bedroom and found an extra dresser. When he opened the door to the adjoining storage space, he groaned. There had been no more room for anything in that back area, so they'd flooded his.

Someone had moved a bunch of stuff from Nonna's down here. His aunts, most likely, making space for the nurse at the expense of their nephew. This was not okay. First, they begged him to stay with his grandmother, then they hired a woman to care for her when they knew he preferred otherwise, and now they'd swamped his sanctuary with the excess?

A note on the counter caught his eye.

Tony —

Sorry we had to put some of Nonna's things in here to make room for Kenna. Promise we'll deal with it soon.

Aunt Gen

His aunts and uncles had big enough houses they could have hauled the stuff up the hill. If it wasn't where Nonna could see it, she likely wouldn't remember she owned it. It wasn't like she'd be poking around the basement for the next couple of months while she recuperated.

Tony needed order. He needed a haven from the intensity of the restaurant. He needed a place that was solely his, where well-meaning relatives didn't move his things around to make room for Nonna's overflow.

Should he be looking for a place to rent? He cringed inside at the thought of taking that on just now. He was too busy for the search, let alone the move. Nonna's was within easy walking distance of the restaurant, and that saved a lot of time and hassle. Besides, once Nonna recovered and the nurse moved out, he'd be required here again. The restaurant would be running more smoothly, and he could focus on Nonna. Maybe help her get rid of some of this stuff permanently.

He had to be patient. At the same time, his aunts needed to know that it was not okay to invade his space.

What was with him today? Although, to be honest, his edginess had been growing for a while. He'd moved to Spokane — to the bosom of his boisterous Italian family — with such high hopes. He'd spent a few months living with Dan Ranta, helping the man care for his kids while their mother was estranged. Tony had used his time to oversee construction at the restaurant and work out details. It had worked out well for both men, but life had moved on. Now

Dan was married and the restaurant was open five nights a week.

That's when the problems had started. He'd moved to Nonna's just a couple of weeks before opening Antonio's. He was just too busy to spend time with her or his cousins.

Stress. Life had become a gigantic ball of stress.

Tony was up for it. It's what he'd signed on for, eyes wide open... but he hadn't expected it to be quite this hard. Being the boss was exhausting. All-encompassing.

Lonely.

There was nothing he could do about that, either. The only people he regularly dealt with were his employees, and he wasn't dumb enough to date one of them, not that anyone had caught his eye.

He locked the door, pulled his tablet out of his messenger bag, and turned out the kitchen light before heading into his bedroom. He'd read a chapter or two of his current fantasy series and call it a night.

3

*K*enna lifted a box out of her hatchback and turned for the house, but someone blocked her path.

"Here, let me get that. How many more do you have?"

Tony. He even sounded like an average nice guy, which ratcheted up her cautionary flags. Maurice had hidden behind nice-guy, too.

"A few." She pointed her chin toward the open vehicle. "I'll be living here for several months, you know."

"I know." His blue eyes assessed her as he took the box. "Sorry about the other day. I was rude, and that's not my usual."

"No problem." She ducked back for a rolling case then followed him up the steps. His hands were full, so she got the door for them both.

He set the box on the dresser in her room then looked around the space, eyes narrowed. "This looks... different."

"It was pretty full of junk. I had them move it all out of here."

"And into my apartment downstairs."

"What? Oh. I'm sorry." She hadn't thought about where it was going. She'd only cared that it disappeared. Then she'd rented a carpet cleaner yesterday and come over to scrub the room from top to bottom.

He shrugged a lithe shoulder. "Not your fault my grand-mother has way too much stuff. Something's got to be done, though. I can't live like this."

A man after her own heart.

Scratch that. Such a man didn't exist. Not that she'd thought Maurice was him, either.

"She does have a lot of stuff." Surely that was safe to admit.

A lopsided grin on Tony's face revealed a dimple amid the scruff on his left cheek.

Kenna stifled the urge to roll her eyes. He was such a cliché. Tall, dark, handsome, blue eyes, and even a dimple. Not that height made much of an impression, since she was above average there herself.

"I'll get the rest of your stuff. Go ahead and start unpacking."

"No need. I can do it."

His eyebrows rose just a little. "So can I, and I was raised with manners."

Like she hadn't been? Which might be truer than she preferred to admit. "Thank you, then."

Tony pivoted out of the room, and she breathed a sigh of relief. First order of business, making up this bed with her own sheets and duvet. She'd stripped the linens yesterday and run them through the wash, so she should also fold everything out of the dryer and put it... where? Not in the basement, apparently.

Kenna rubbed both temples in an attempt to ward off the incoming headache. She couldn't tackle the old lady's hoard without the help and support of the family. Sounded like Tony, at least, would be on her side. Fat lot of good that would do since they assured her he was never home. Then what was he doing here now?

He came in and set a stack of smaller boxes beside the door.

She would choose not to notice the ripple of his muscles as he did so. "Thanks."

"No problem. A couple more trips should do it." He ran his fingers through short brown hair. "You're keeping your old place?"

Kenna straightened as she met his gaze then bit back her ready retort.

He backed away a little. "Just a friendly question."

"Of course. I'm not stupid enough to think I'm staying here for more than a couple of months. Your grandmother's doctors expect a complete recovery, although not a quick one at her age. One of the nurses in my unit just left her husband and needs a place to live while she figures things out, so she's moved into my apartment."

"I see." He turned and headed back out of the room.

Kenna tucked her bottom sheet over the padded mattress. She had the duvet spread when Tony returned with the next load and the pillows plumped before he brought in the final items, which included her garment bag. She unzipped it and carried several dresses on hangers over to the closet.

She flicked a glance at the guy still standing in the doorway. "Thanks."

"You're welcome." But he didn't move.

"I'm sure you have a lot of things to do." Hint, hint.

"I was just going to fix myself some lunch. Join me?"

In his overcrowded basement space? Not a chance. "No, thank you."

"I'd like us to get along."

"Sure, no problem." She hung the rest of her clothing and spaced out the hangers so every item had a little room to breathe without getting wrinkled.

"Are you always this prickly, or is this a special occasion?"

"Prickly?" Kenna turned to face him, hands on her hips. "I'm a nurse. I'm here to take care of your grandmother, not make cozy friends for tea."

"There's no reason you can't do both."

The man was persistent, she'd give him that. "Maybe I don't want to. Maybe my job is all that's important to me."

Tony winced.

Kenna didn't think she'd been particularly cutting or witty to cause that reaction, but the fact remained that she was on a mission. She'd gotten derailed by Maurice — how had that happened, anyway? — and wouldn't again. No more little-old-man outpatients for her. Men of any age were dangerous, probably from newborn on up. Not that she'd ever be around a newborn. She wasn't having any of her own, that was for sure.

Tony backed into the hallway, and Kenna breathed a sigh of relief until she heard the fridge door. Then clanking pans. What on earth was he doing in her kitchen? His grandmother's kitchen, that is. Not his. Maybe if she ignored him, he'd go away. This was likely an anomaly. Tomorrow was the big family work day — and didn't they have their job cut out for themselves? — then she'd pick up the old woman from the rehab center, and their new life would begin.

She'd be too busy cleaning this house and nursing the invalid to worry about the grandson who seemed unable to stay in his place. He'd get the picture, or she'd talk to Grace Santoro, the woman who appeared to be in charge of this clan.

The stench of cooking fish wafted down the hallway. Ugh. Kenna closed the bedroom door and finished unpacking, aware of every sound from the kitchen. The interior door didn't block odors all that well, either. The fishiness was joined by garlic and tomatoes.

Didn't Tony have someplace to be? A restaurant to run? Anything? Anywhere?

THE HOUSE HUMMED WITH ACTIVITY. Tony could hear the buzz of his uncles' saws and their laughing banter through the closed front door as they built a ramp to accommodate Nonna's wheelchair. She was going to hate relying on that thing.

In the living room, his aunts washed windows, dusted knickknacks, sorted through Nonna's knitting projects, and rearranged furniture. They'd better not haul anything else down to his space.

Down the hallway, electric screwdrivers buzzed as Marco and Alex installed grab bars in Nonna's bathroom.

Out the kitchen window, several of Tony's cousins weeded the garden. Jasmine had picked four heaping baskets of vine-ripened tomatoes. She and Peter operated an organic box program, supplying dozens of households with fresh produce. Tony'd love to get Antonio's on their list, but the restaurant needed far more than Bridgeview Backyards could supply at this stage.

Jasmine came in the back door with an armful of lavender, the heady fragrance nearly overwhelming the pungent pasta sauce Tony had put on to simmer. She gave an appreciative sniff in his direction. "Ooh, that smells good."

He grinned at her. "So does that. What are you going to do with all that?"

She laughed. "Do you think Nonna will guess that I'm trying to destress her if there are bouquets in every room?"

"She might. But then, she shouldn't have planted so much of the stuff."

"I like the way you think. Want some downstairs? You look like you could stand some tension relief, too."

"Who, me?" Not that his innocent words would put Jasmine off for long. "Sure, I'll take some. Not only that, but I could do a lavender panna cotta down at the restaurant one night this week."

"Mmm. Sounds yum. There's plenty left in that border, and more in the community garden next door. Just watch out for bees."

"Yes, Mother."

Jasmine wrinkled her nose at him. "Well, I wouldn't want you to get stung. They're busy little bees these days, storing up honey while the sun shines."

"Which you're going to steal from them."

"But of course. It's what beekeepers do. We've got a lot of clients at Bridgeview Backyards who are looking for local honey. Really helps with seasonal allergies."

"Then it's a good thing you have so many yards you can put beehives in."

"Sure is. We're not placing them where there are young kids, of course, but lots of our older homeowners love watching the bees in their gardens as much as they enjoy visiting birds. Total win-win."

A baby cried from the other room, and Jasmine turned that direction on full alert. "Lillian's awake. I'm amazed she slept this long with all the hubbub."

"Where is she?"

"I tucked her bassinet in Nonna's sewing room. Figured she'd be out of the way there. What else can they cram in that room?"

Tony shook his head with a grin. "Someone needs to do an intervention. You know that, right?"

She placed her hand on her chest and widened her eyes. "An intervention for me? You shouldn't have." The baby whimpered again then quieted.

"Ha. No. For Nonna and her hoarding ways. I'd say there's no better time than now while she's incapacitated."

"Because she won't be able to fight us off? You're sneaky."

"Everyone will be here more than usual, too." Intruding on Tony's downtime. Maybe he'd need a fresh bouquet of lavender every week. He lowered his voice. "I'm willing to bet the nurse would be happy to get in on it. Have you seen what she allowed to remain in the guest room? Or maybe you had a hand in it?"

His cousin shook his head. "Mom told me they cleaned out all but a couple of pieces of furniture, though, plus all the junk."

"Did she tell you where they put it all? It's now gracing my space downstairs."

Jasmine wrinkled her nose. "Nice solution."

"Yeah, for them. Not for me. Seriously, someone needs to get ruthless."

"So this is going to be your fight?"

Tony sighed. "I don't know. I feel like I don't know Nonna well enough to take that on. You guys all grew up in and out of this house, but I only visited from Idaho a few times a year. I'm still finding my place."

"Aw, Tony, I'm glad you're here. Here, as in with Nonna, but also, just that you're around, and we can all get to know each other as adults."

"Yeah, me, too. There's not much I can really do for Nonna, though. Especially with Kenna around."

"Nonna still needs her family around her. Just do what you've always done, and keep things as normal as possible."

"I'll try, but Kenna really doesn't like me."

Jasmine chuckled. "What's not to like?"

"You'd have to ask her, because I have no clue." That wasn't completely true. He'd been on the rude side when they first met, but he'd apologized. It was on her that she'd flipped off his effort at amends and continued to be abrasive. Tony lowered his voice. "You know her better than any of us. Do you really trust her around Nonna?"

"I don't know her well at all. I mean, she was married to Nathan's dad, but not in a time period where I had anything to do with them. Maurice passed away before Nathan and I got serious with each other."

"What if there's something she's hiding?"

"Like what? She stuck it out with Maurice for six years, Tony. He was a mean, belligerent man, but she didn't divorce him." Jasmine held up a hand. "And she had to know there wasn't going to be a big inheritance to make it worth her while. She didn't even get the house, because Maurice never changed his will to include her. Nathan tried to give it to her and she refused. It was chock-full of bad memories for him. We had to do a pretty serious remodel before he could relax and call it home."

"Maybe it held bad memories for her, too."

"I wouldn't doubt it. No, whatever is going on with Makenna, I think she's above board."

Tony let out a long breath. "If you're sure."

"She really rubs you the wrong way, does she?"

He rolled his eyes. "Ya think?"

Jasmine leaned closer, amusement dancing in her eyes. "Maybe you're resisting an attraction to her."

"Get real, Jasmine. I wouldn't be interested in her if she were the last woman on the planet."

A cough sounded from over at the entrance to the living room. Kenna stood there, hands on both hips, her frosty gaze pinned on his.

Uh oh. He'd said exactly how he felt, but he hadn't meant for her to overhear him.

Kenna raised haughty brows at Jasmine. "Your mom thought you were still outside. She asked me to let you know the baby is awake and changed."

"Thanks. I'll go get Lillian right now." Jasmine wiggled her fingers in Tony's direction as she left the room. No eye contact.

Thanks, cuz.

"Just so you know, the feeling is mutual." Kenna's chin tipped upward. "I'm a nurse, and this is only a job to me. Save your conspiracy theories for someone else."

"I didn't mean—"

Her narrowed eyes silenced him as she stared him down.

"I'll just finish making lunch for everyone, then. I hope you enjoy spaghetti and meatballs Santoro style."

"I had lunch before I came over. I'm leaving shortly to pick up your grandmother from the rehab center. I hope the ramp will be completed by the time I get back. Rehab needs the bed for someone else."

"Of course. Thank you for taking care of her."

She appraised him coolly. "It's my job."

4

_T_he house still buzzed with family when Kenna arrived with Mrs. Santoro a couple of hours later. Tony had left the kitchen spotless with the dishwasher humming. At least the guy took cleanliness seriously. At least he had a job that took him away from the house.

Not for the first time, she resolutely blocked the conversation she'd overheard earlier. She didn't care what he thought of her. Her job was all about the man's grandmother. It had nothing to do with him, other than that he lived rather too close.

Mrs. Santoro's shrewd gaze took in the rearranged living room, but she was easily distracted by her sons, daughters-in-law, and grandchildren waiting to welcome her home. It was touching, really. The old lady came across a bit crusty, but there was no denying the love between them all.

Kenna had never experienced that kind of affection. Even as a child, she'd known she couldn't count on anyone else to look out for her. Still couldn't.

Jasmine leaned down to give her grandmother a gentle

touch and a kiss on her weathered cheek. "Welcome home, Nonna. I'm so glad you're feeling better."

"It's good to be home." She seemed ready to say more, but pursed her lips.

"Can I fix you a coffee, Mamma?" asked Genevera. "Francesca and I made biscotti. Tieri even helped." She smiled down at her eight-year-old granddaughter.

Baking biscotti in the heat of August demonstrated true love, though Gen's house was likely air-conditioned, unlike Kenna's third-floor apartment.

"Please. What they call coffee in the hospital is only colored water."

True, that.

Gen caught Kenna's eye. "Are you familiar with Marietta's espresso maker?"

"No?"

"Come along, then."

What if Mrs. Santoro needed her and she wasn't here? Not that any one of these people wouldn't help their matriarch. She leaned down to the old woman's shoulder. "Excuse me a moment?"

Mrs. Santoro fluttered her fingers then winced. "Go."

"Mamma is quite particular about her coffee," Gen said when Kenna followed her into the kitchen. "Most of us have regular drip coffeemakers we use every day, but not Mamma. She'll use hers for a crowd, but she prefers to brew each cup fresh with her stovetop coffee maker."

"So, instant coffee is out of the question?"

Genevera laughed as she held up a battered aluminum pot. "You're funny."

Kenna hadn't meant to be. She usually fixed herself

instant at home. Takeout from a coffee shop worked if she was on the go.

"Fill the bottom with filtered water from the fridge dispenser." Gen demonstrated. "Then a few cranks of this handle will get enough grounds to fill the filter funnel."

No way. This was a lot of work for a single cup of coffee. But they were paying her well to keep their matriarch happy. If coffee made in this contraption was the way to her heart, Kenna would learn it. She pointed at the wooden grinder. "I thought espresso required a finer grind." Not that she knew anything.

"That's what they would have you think, but a moka maker like this one can get clogged if it's too fine."

"Mocha?"

"Moka with a k. See, you fill the funnel to the top, set it in the bottom chamber, and screw the top on here. Not too tight." Gen set it on the stove and turned the burner on.

Kenna eyed it. "That seems like it could explode with heat."

Gen smiled. "Not unless you leave it too long. Hear that? It's coming to a boil already."

The bubbling was replaced by a gurgling sound then Gen snapped off the burner and held up the pot. "Ready to serve. Mamma prefers one of the pottery mugs from the rack over here. They're her favorites." Gen poured the thick, strong-smelling brew into a red mug decorated with hearts and held it out to Kenna. "Just like that. I'll get the biscotti."

"No sugar? Cream?"

"Nope. Black as a moonless night."

"How many of these does she drink a day?"

Gen arranged stacks of biscotti on a plate. "No more than five or six, I wouldn't think."

"That's a lot of caffeine."

"She has her last cup after dinner. It doesn't seem to keep her awake."

The old lady was hardier than she. Kenna couldn't even sniff coffee past mid-afternoon if she wanted to sleep.

"Oh, I need to leave a couple of pieces for Tony. Almond is his favorite flavor." Gen slipped two pieces of biscotti onto a smaller plate. "He was sorry he couldn't stay until his nonna arrived, but he's so busy with the new restaurant."

The less said about him, the better.

"Such a dear boy. I do hope you will get along well with him."

Makenna raised her eyebrows. "I'm sure we'll see very little of each other. He is, as you say, extremely busy."

"He's never too busy to spend time with his nonna." Gen smiled indulgently. "Although he seems to be too busy for a social life. I don't think that's healthy. Do you?"

This was Kenna's problem how? "Everyone makes choices. Now, is this ready for Mrs. Santoro?" As she said it, she realized she was speaking to Mrs. Santoro, and there were several more in the house at the moment.

"Call her Marietta. If she hasn't insisted yet, she will soon."

It would be so much easier to keep her distance, to remember the nurse-patient relationship, if she kept up the formal address. She wasn't here to make friends with any of the family members. Not Marietta, not Genevera or Jasmine, and definitely not Tony.

The goal was a good recommendation to get the job

offer she wanted later in the fall. The timing should be just about exactly right. After that, she'd never need to look at a Santoro again if she didn't want to. For now, though, they were a major part of her life, and she'd definitely do her best to care for Marietta.

Kenna followed Genevera into the other room where the family sat and chatted with each other. Mrs. Santoro grimaced slightly as she shifted in her chair a minuscule amount.

"Are you all right?" Kenna set the coffee mug on a nearby table and squatted at the old lady's knee. She glanced at her watch. "It's a little too early for another round of pain medications. Perhaps you'd like to lie down?"

"But my family—"

"They all live in the neighborhood. They can visit any time." Kenna rose and looked around the noisy room. "She needs to rest." Grasping the handles, she propelled the wheelchair down the short hallway and parked it beside the new hospital-style bed.

Kenna spared a thought for what had happened to the regular one. Probably cramping Tony's style in the basement. Well, that wasn't her problem. She drew back the duvet and settled Mrs. Santoro gently in bed. "Would you like the curtains open or shut? And I'll go get your coffee and one of the biscotti your daughter-in-law made."

"Open. To see the birds."

The way her eyelids drooped, Kenna doubted the birds would hold her attention. No problem. The curtains could remain open anyway. She hustled down the short hallway to retrieve the coffee and a napkin with biscotti.

Jasmine stopped her with a touch on the arm. "Thank you," she said simply.

Kenna raised her eyebrows. "For...?"

"For making sure Nonna's needs are met ahead of everyone else's."

"It's my job."

"And you're doing it well. She's in good hands."

Kenna blinked. An overture from the woman who would have been Maurice's daughter-in-law had he lived? Unexpected.

༄ ⸲ ⸲

DUDE. Marley loves me! We're back together!

Tony blinked at his cousin Alex's text before sagging back against his pillow. Seven o'clock. One of the hazards of working until past midnight every night then needing time to unwind was trying to sleep when other people were already up and at it.

I'm happy for you, he texted back. Mostly happy. Tony didn't know Marley well, but she and Alex had been on and off for most of the summer. They were polar opposites. Instead of seeing how complementary that made them, they'd clashed over it. So, yeah, good for them working things out. There'd doubtless be another set of Santoro wedding bells coming up in the next few months. There'd been a whole raft of them in the past year or two, and Peter and Sadie's wedding was set for Thanksgiving weekend.

Why hadn't he thought of that before deciding this was the perfect time to move close to his extended family? But if he'd waited another year or five, it wouldn't have been any better. Fewer weddings, perhaps, but more babies.

Tony liked kids. Loved rough-housing with his sister's two. Had reveled in living with Dan Ranta and helping care for his three over last winter while Dan worked things out with the children's mother, Dixie. Enjoyed his cousins' babies and toddlers and even Marco's school-age boys.

He'd put having a family on hold indefinitely with his choice to launch a brand-new restaurant. He knew that. Had known it at the time. Antonio's simply took too much time and energy. Tony couldn't run the restaurant and meet the needs of a family.

That didn't keep him from wanting it.

"Can't have it both ways, Santoro," he mumbled, swinging his legs over the side of the bed.

Overhead, hard-heeled shoes clopped across the hardwood floor. Tony stared at the ceiling, narrowing his gaze as the shoes retraced their steps. Then again.

Didn't the nurse know he worked late? Who wore footwear like that in the house? Must be those stupid heels. He'd never seen her in casual shoes. Maybe he should suggest she buy some. His aunts and uncles were certainly paying her enough.

He stumbled into the suite's tiny kitchenette and prepped his coffee steamer. This was how Nonna liked hers, too. Had Kenna ever seen one of these contraptions before? Maybe he should go upstairs and make sure Nonna had a decent cup of coffee. He could fix her breakfast, too, if she hadn't eaten already. And there was the to-go container he'd brought home from the restaurant last night. She'd like that for her lunch.

Just because she had a live-in companion right now didn't mean Tony should shirk his duties.

His moka machine gurgled as the pressurized water passed through the coffee grounds. He removed it from the element and poured the brew. Ah, bliss. The best coffee anywhere on the planet.

Tony took a quick shower, dressed in shorts and a T-shirt, snagged the takeout container, and headed up the outside steps. He stepped through the French doors into the breakfast room, set the container down, and walked through to the living room.

His grandmother sat in a wheelchair near the window overlooking the street while the nurse sat beside her, sharing a magazine. They looked cozy, but since when did nurses wear floral knee-length dresses and three-inch heels to care for someone?

"Good morning, Nonna!" Tony crossed the space and crouched at her side.

Kenna gasped, nearly dropping the magazine. "You scared the living daylights out of me, walking in like that without even knocking."

Seriously? He angled his head and looked over at her. "I live here."

Her hands flapped. "But you don't live *here*."

"Same thing." He turned to Nonna and grasped her hands lightly. "I'm sorry I wasn't home when you returned yesterday. How are you doing?"

"Frustrated," she mumbled.

He could see that. "I'd be frustrated, too, having someone different in my space all the time."

"I'm her nurse."

"I was talking to my grandmother." Tony patted Nonna's hands. "How about if I fix you some breakfast?"

"She's eaten."

Tony huffed a sigh and looked over at the nurse. "How about letting Nonna and me have a conversation?"

"Fine." She glared at him, pivoted on her heels, and strode toward the hallway. Click. Click. Click.

"Another thing," he called after her.

Makenna turned so quickly her dress flared around her knees for a quick second. She crossed her arms and stared at him. "Yes?"

"Could you find softer soled shoes to wear around the house? I can hear every step you take in those things downstairs."

An eyebrow quirked. "Anything else, Mr. Santoro?"

He arched his own brows. "That's everything for now, Ms. *Johnson*."

If anything, her shoes made even more noise as she clomped down the hallway and into her room. The door shut firmly behind her.

Great. Now she was mad at him. Tony sighed as he turned back to Nonna. "Is she treating you all right? Because if she's not..."

Nonna offered a wan smile. "Frustrated from pain, not from her. She's doing a fine job."

Oh. Well, he'd handled that like a champ, hadn't he? "Do you need some pain meds?" He'd have to make nice with the nurse to ask for them. He wasn't dumb enough to assume he could just grab Nonna a couple of Advil and call it a day. That would bring down the Wrath of Makenna, and he'd deserve every bit of it.

"Can't have them yet."

"Okay." Man, he hated to see her suffer, though. "Coffee? Breakfast?" Anything?

"I've eaten."

Tony shot a glance down the hallway, but the nurse's door was firmly closed. "What did she make you?"

"Bacon and eggs. Overdone."

"I'll do better, Nonna. What time do you want breakfast tomorrow?" It likely had something to do with the timing of her medications. He should get up to speed on that.

Nonna closed her eyes and shook her head slightly.

"What can I do?" He hated feeling helpless. Hated that Nonna had fallen that day. She'd been at Marley's house teaching her to sew vintage tea towels into curtains, gone outside, tripped over a chicken, and fallen against a planter on the back step. She'd broken two ribs and her right arm, but the biggest worry came from the hairline fractures in her pelvic bones.

"Nothing, dear boy."

That was not an okay answer. Tony was a take-charge kind of guy, and there was nothing worse than being powerless. Nothing worse... except for having to trust a snippy woman who rubbed him the wrong way to do things he couldn't.

5

_K_enna knelt in front of the open closet with her shoe rack across the bottom. And here she'd thought she had variety. Black, white, beige, pink, turquoise, purple, leopard print. Some with narrower or taller heels than others. Some closed-toe and some open.

All of them had hard soles and heels, and His Royal Highness was bothered by her footsteps. He might as well tell her she was too heavy while he was at it. After all, a tiny woman would make less noise. Not that she was fat. She worked too hard to maintain her figure to get that way, but she had distinct hips and a bust. She was tall, and she definitely weighed more than a little snip of a thing like Jasmine.

Kenna pulled her nursing shoes out of the back and looked at them in distaste. They'd be quieter, sure, but they looked terrible with a dress. She shuddered at the thought, but the one of her in jeans — or, heaven help her, shorts — was equally unimaginable. She'd worked hard to build her confidence and her wardrobe after Maurice, and those shoes were only for the hospital.

The new Makenna Johnson wouldn't allow any man to tell her what to wear. What to look like. She sat back on her heels and stared at her collection. So why was she contemplating softer shoes to make her client's grandson happy? She should simply tell him sorry-not-sorry. It wasn't her fault he lived in the basement and worked until late.

On the other hand, there was no reason to be mean, either. Alienating Tony wasn't in her best interests if she wanted a good recommendation from the family, and she did. Besides, she liked Marietta. Maybe she could pull off leggings and long tunics with nursing shoes and not cringe too much when she looked in the mirror.

An excuse to go shopping was never completely unwelcome. The problem was letting a man dictate what she could or could not wear. Maybe tomorrow she'd see if she could get away for a couple of hours. One thing, she'd never ask Tony Santoro to keep an eye on his grandmother for her. Not for this reason, nor any other.

A light tap sounded on her door. "Kenna?"

She stared at the door for a second before rising and crossing the space to open it.

Tony stood on the other side wearing a worried frown. "Nonna would like to lie down, and I'm not sure of the best way to help her."

"That's my job." She managed a smile — *no more alienation, remember?* — and brushed past him. Her footsteps echoed as she strode to the living room. *Fine, Mr. Santoro; you'll get your wish.* She squatted beside the wheelchair. "Ready for a rest, Mrs. Santoro?"

"Call me Marietta. Please."

No longer the bossy woman Maurice had loathed, the old lady was frail. Her voice, thin. "All right, Marietta. Let's tuck you in for a nap." She rose, but Tony grasped the handles of the wheelchair before she could get there. What part of her job didn't he understand?

He raised his eyebrows at her as he pushed the chair into motion.

Kenna followed, glaring at his back and the ripple of his gray T-shirt as he turned into the master bedroom. The T-shirt hung untucked over his denim shorts, not that she was checking out his backside or his tanned, sculpted calves. Or his bare feet. At least his toenails were trimmed.

"What do I do next?" he asked over his shoulder.

"I've got it."

"I want to know how."

She managed not to huff her frustration as she set the brakes and eased Marietta's transition to the bed.

"Can I get you anything, Nonna?" Tony leaned over the pillow, his tanned hand cupping his grandmother's cheek.

Kenna needed to cut the guy some slack. They were on the same team. He obviously cared about his grandmother, and Kenna was coming to feel the same.

"Coffee," the old woman murmured.

"I'll get it." Kenna turned toward the door.

"Tony can."

Her eyebrows flew up. "I know how your contraption works. Genevera showed me yesterday."

"She asked me." Tony marched out of the room.

Was that a wisp of a smile on the old woman's face? Kenna wasn't certain. All she could do was follow the man into the kitchen and plead her case. She'd already made one cup of the pressurized coffee today. It hadn't exploded or anything. Mrs. Santoro hadn't complained about it. She'd even thanked her.

Tony was already tapping the spent grounds into the compost — who knew that was a thing? — then ground more beans and refilled the filter.

Kenna filled the bottom reservoir from the fridge dispenser then stood by while Tony assembled the gadget. "It would save a lot of time to just make a pot of coffee." She pointed at the drip machine on the far counter. "I could reheat cups for her in the microwave whenever she wanted one."

"Sacrilege."

Her hands found her hips. "Excuse me? Millions of people use those coffee makers. They do the job."

He turned the element on and leaned against the counter facing her, his arms and ankles crossed. "That's not how she likes her coffee." His grin poked his dimple into action.

Didn't the guy ever shave? Not that she cared if he had to wear a beard net in his restaurant kitchen. His problem, not hers. On the other hand, he must shave, or the scruff would be longer.

Tony chuckled.

Her gaze flew to his eyes. "What's so funny?"

"You. You're staring at me like you've never seen a guy before. Pretty sure that's not the case."

"I wasn't staring."

His eyebrows rose, and his blue eyes laughed at her.

Okay, she *had* been staring. She pointed at the coffee machine as it began to bubble. "Your aunt did show me how to use that yesterday."

"Cool."

"So I don't need your help."

"Let's get one thing perfectly clear, okay? This is my grandmother we're talking about. You can't ban me from seeing her or doing little things to help her, so just loosen up a little, will you?"

"I'm being paid—"

"I know. There are plenty of things you can do that I can't. But I do have days off, and I'm around most mornings, and I *will* come upstairs whenever I want to." The laughter had left his eyes. "I hope that's acceptable to you. If it isn't, just deal with it."

Well. Kenna broke from his gaze then noticed a cardboard container sitting on the counter. It certainly had not been there earlier. "What's that?"

"Leftover pasta primavera. I brought it from the restaurant for Nonna's lunch."

"I'm paid to do the cooking."

Tony rolled his eyes. "Have you not heard a thing I said? I'm a chef. Food is how I take care of people. I'm not bringing her three meals a day, just an occasional treat. Calm down already."

Calm down? He was ordering her to relax?

The coffee maker gurgled, and Kenna lunged for it before Tony could. She poured the brew into a mug and turned toward the hallway. "Thanks for your help." He'd be smart enough to read the bitterness in her voice.

⁂

THAT WOMAN HAD a chip on her shoulder the size of the Pacific Northwest. Man.

Tony tucked the container in the fridge and let himself

out onto the back patio where he sucked in a long breath. Someone, probably Jasmine, had hung several bunches of lavender beneath the grape arbor. She had to have done it for relaxation purposes, since drying it in the light wasn't optimal for use in sachets or food. It was going to take a whole lot more lavender than this to destress him, but bless his cousin for trying.

Maybe he should go down to the restaurant. None of his staff would be in yet, so he could experiment in the quiet kitchen for a while. Maybe play with his idea for a simple tortelli with a lavender and parmesan filling. If it seemed promising, he could assign Oriana to making a large batch of pasta on Friday afternoon and offer it as a special that evening. And if that went well, he could try again another time with a gluten-free dough.

His spirits lifted slightly.

With a chuckle, he tapped his knuckles lightly against the nearest lavender bundle. Maybe the stuff was working already.

Someone laughed. "Did you seriously just fist-bump the lavender?"

Tony whirled to see Jasmine coming through the gate from the community garden next door, wearing a baby carrier on her back. "I did. Is Lillian awake?"

Jasmine shook her head. "I think she's out, but I can't see for sure." She turned sideways.

He ran his finger down the sleeping baby's soft cheek and her lips pursed. "She's dreaming of food. True Santoro."

"Or Hamelin." Jasmine grinned at him. "How are things going?"

The brief moment of euphoria popped like a burst bubble. "You don't even want to know."

"Try me."

Tony thumbed over his shoulder toward the house. "She's completely impossible."

"I have a feeling you're not talking about Nonna."

He rolled his eyes. "Too right."

"So here's the question."

"Yeah?"

"Is she taking good care of Nonna?"

"She burned breakfast."

"Well, that's a capital crime, for sure," Jasmine said blandly.

"It pretty much is. How much finesse does it take to not burn bacon and eggs?"

"This is only the first day. Maybe she's used to a stove with slower elements."

He grunted. "Maybe." And his cousin was right. It was only the first day. If the nurse burned breakfast every day for a week, he'd have more of a case.

"Is Nonna up? I was going to pop in for a quick visit."

"We just put her to bed for a nap."

Jasmine's eyebrows rose. "We?"

"Okay, Kenna did it, and I watched."

She twitched a grin at him. "So hard to admit when there's something you can't do, huh, buddy?"

"I could do it. I just didn't know how. I'll know for next time."

"Let her do her job, Tony."

"She seems to think her job includes me staying out of sight and out of mind. That's not going to happen."

"But do you have to push her?"

"Hey, that's not fair." Tony took a step back and glowered at his cousin. "Who said anything about pushing her? I want to know she's doing a good job. I have Nonna's best interests at heart."

"My mom and the aunts are certain Makenna's the right person for the job."

"They're not here all day like I am."

"Listen to yourself."

"What?" He glared at Jasmine. "Okay, I'm only around in the mornings and weekends. Or what passes for weekends in my world. But, still. I'm here more than the aunts are."

"What really bugs you about her? And I don't mean burned bacon, because you didn't like her long before that happened."

Tony glanced over his shoulder, but Kenna wasn't visible through the French doors. Having her overhear his conversation with Jasmine once was enough. It didn't need to happen again. He ran his fingers through his hair. "I don't know. She drives me crazy."

Jasmine shook her head. "I'm not buying that you don't know. It was an instant aversion. There had to be something."

"She looks so... perfect. Like she has an agenda to uphold."

"Perfect?" Jasmine's eyes widened. "You think Makenna looks perfect?"

"That's not what I meant."

"It's what you said."

He had, hadn't he? "I meant her figure. And her clothes. And her heels. Who nurses an old woman with perfect hair and makeup and heels?"

Jasmine looked at him thoughtfully. "Is there any reason she shouldn't? I mean, dressing up isn't my style, but why does it bug you if it's hers? Does it prevent her from doing her job?"

Women always stuck up for each other. "You asked. I answered."

"Are you attracted to her?"

Tony reared back, staring at his cousin. "Are you some kind of crazy? Not a chance."

"Because if you are, you should know that she's older than you by about five years."

"Who cares?"

Jasmine smirked. "I don't. It's just information."

"You... I can't believe what you're implying. Because there's nothing to back up your supposition. I'm totally not interested in her that way. Did you miss the part where she drives me crazy?"

"Methinks you protest too much."

"Methinks you have rocks in your head. I hear them rattling from over here."

"I live to interfere." She chuckled. "They don't call me Nonna Junior for nothing."

Tony narrowed his eyes as he stared at his cousin. Had Nonna been grimacing from pain when she sent him to make coffee or had that been a smirk? Was Nonna pitting him against Kenna on purpose?

hy did this crazy family keep bringing lavender into the house? She liked flowers as much as the next girl, but there were other blooms out in the yard. Through the fence, Kenna could see a colorful border — distinctly more vibrant than purple — in the community garden next door.

It was mostly Jasmine, who dropped by every couple of days to see her grandmother, but the aunts weren't above it, either. If they didn't bring more in, they rearranged the existing arrangements and moved them from one room to another. They could just stay out of hers.

Kenna wasn't stupid. She knew lavender's reputation for alleviating stress. Okay, so there was a lot of tension in this house, and it wasn't all her. Mrs. Santoro was visibly in pain, which made her a bit grumpy. All the visitors — a regular parade of them — seemed to give the old lady a pass. Maybe this amount of irritability was normal for her. How would Kenna know? She'd had as little as possible to do with this family before now.

And no one knocked. Ever. Right now, Kenna scrubbed toddler fingerprints off the living room window and watched Winnie turn up the sidewalk.

She strolled inside a moment later, wearing a pensive smile. "Hi, Kenna. How's our patient today?"

"Resting." Mrs. Santoro found lying down to be less painful than sitting up. "But she'll be happy to see you, I'm sure."

Winnie fidgeted with the hem of her striped top. "Kenna... how did you manage when Maurice died?"

What? Kenna's mouth gaped.

"Today it's been two years since Al's accident. I never expected to be a widow, at least not until I was old and gray."

"It was sudden for you." She remembered hearing about it.

"He lingered for a few days, but he never regained consciousness." Winnie's voice quieted. "It was very difficult."

"Maurice was ill for a long time, declining gradually. I had more time to grow accustomed to the situation. Plus, he was thirty years older, so I always assumed he'd die before me."

"I'm not sure which would be harder. It must have been tough watching the man you loved fade away."

Had she loved Maurice? She must have, once. Sort of. He'd always been difficult, but Kenna was no quitter. Besides, she'd tended to believe the things he said about her were true. Three years later, she could see they weren't. Not all of them, anyway.

"Have you thought about remarrying?"

"No." Kenna narrowed her gaze at Winnie. "I never

want to be dependent on anyone else ever again." Especially a man.

"Sometimes well-meaning friends encourage me to consider dating. Al and I had been married almost twenty-five years. I don't know what dating looks like these days for people my age. I'll be fifty this year."

Was she hearing Winnie right? Like she actually kind of wanted to? Kenna scrubbed at one last smudge. Dafne had brought two-year-old Gavin over this morning, and the kid had smeared his nose and peanut-butter-laden fingers all over the bottom of that window. Yuck.

Kenna sat back on her heels, easier with tennis shoes than pumps, and looked over at Winnie. "I'm thirty-three, but the idea of spending the rest of my life single isn't that daunting. Nursing is the perfect career for me." At least, it would be when she finally nailed down a permanent position.

"You don't get lonely?"

"Not really." Having people around only meant she became dependent on them in some way.

"I do." Winnie sounded wistful. "My kids are great, but they're growing up. Two have left home. Dominic was in medical school in Seattle even before his dad passed away. Brittany's done with college and shares an apartment with her cousin Ava. Gabriella will be home for a bit yet as she's attending community college. Now Landon's in his senior year, and Michael's a teenager. Time sure flies."

Kenna had seen Landon around some as he was friends with Maurice's youngest son, Jason. Both teens worked for Jasmine and Peter's community-supported agriculture business, Bridgeview Backyards. Jason had given her a cool nod the other day when he and Landon had harvested boxes of

Mrs. Santoro's tomatoes and herbs. His attitude had improved remarkably in the intervening years.

"Maybe you need a new job or career." Kenna refocused on Winnie. "Work keeps my mind off things like that." Not completely, but it helped.

"I don't need the money. Al left me fairly well set up, and I like volunteering in the community and at the school. Though that will be different now with Michael in high school. How did that happen?" She shook her head with a nervous smile.

Kenna had no idea. She'd never given birth. Never even been pregnant, and never would. Even Maurice had realized he didn't need any more kids to turn loose on society. Only Nathan had turned out okay, and he'd taken fourteen-year-old Jason under his wing when Maurice died. Maybe the boy would become an asset to society yet, unlike the middle two boys, Ryan and Conner.

Watching little Gavin this morning, Kenna had been all too aware of Connor's features stamped on the toddler's face, even though Maurice's son had as little to do with his child as he could. Maurice's neglect of his own boys had far-reaching effects.

Kenna eyed Winnie. She couldn't imagine not having a fulfilling career to fall back on. She hadn't worked during her marriage to Maurice. In retrospect, she should have told him where to stuff his ideologies. Or been smart enough not to get talked into that quickie Vegas wedding. Six years of her life wasted.

"I volunteer at Blessings Under the Bridge on Wednesday evenings, and I watch little ones during Kass Ferguson's weekly cooking club." Winnie looked at her curiously. "Didn't I see you there once?"

"I went one time. It wasn't really my thing." The food had been good, and it had been nice having meals in the freezer for a while, but hanging out amid a bunch of people who knew and liked each other had soured her. Of course, now she lived in the heart of the community, at least for a couple of months.

Winnie smiled. "I guess it can't be everyone's thing."

Neither could sweet romance.

"How may we pray for you, Tony?"

He looked at the men surrounding the table in the back corner of Bridgeview Bakery and Bistro. Friends. Neighbors. Cousins. He'd attended a similar group in Arcadia Valley during his years there but, of course, minus the relatives.

"Continue to pray for our staffing needs at Antonio's. Also, my grandmother's recovery."

Alex leaned on the table. "Isn't Nonna healing well?"

"As well as can be expected, I guess." What Tony really prayed for was a miracle so that Kenna's services would no longer be required. If that was selfish, so be it.

"We can offer thanks for the safe arrival of Jacob and Eden's twins," put in Logan.

Wade Roper nodded. "Yes!"

"Prayers for my brother Basil," added Alex. "He's coming home next weekend for Nonna's birthday party. He and Dominic are driving out together."

Tony hadn't realized those two cousins had anything to do with each other, though they both lived in Seattle. Dominic attended medical school at the University of

Washington, while Basil waited tables at the Fireweed, the restaurant where Tony and his buddy Levi Esteban had gotten their start after culinary school.

"We're constantly praying for Basil," Peter said. "I'm sure God has a plan for him yet."

Myles Sheridan looked around the table. "Is the birthday party still on? Is Marietta up for it?"

"It's not every day someone turns eighty." Peter grinned. "The aunts figure it will be a good distraction for her."

Tony did a mental scan of the family tree. "Rob and Bren are coming in from Helena. My parents will be here from Galena Landing. So will my sister's family. I think everyone needs to see for themselves that Nonna is okay after her fall."

"Where are your folks staying?" asked Peter.

"With Uncle Ray and Aunt Grace."

"Oh, right. Makenna has the bedroom they usually sleep in," put in Nathan. "How's that going?"

Now all the guys were looking at him. What could he say that wasn't incriminating? Jasmine's teasing words from a couple of days back rang in his mind. "I don't think Nonna has any complaints, except maybe food."

Nathan grinned. "Thankfully, that's something you can help with, right?"

Tony tried to muffle his snort. "Not as easy as you might think." He waved a hand around the table. "I don't want to distract us from prayer time. A lot of you guys need to head off to work soon."

"Anyone need a coffee refill?" Hailey North, one of Bridgeview Bakery and Bistro's owners stood behind Tony's chair, holding a carafe.

"Please." Tony leaned aside. He knew why six in the

morning was the best time for this men's gathering — and was thankful Hailey opened early for them on Thursdays — but it seriously impinged on his sleep.

"Want anything in it?" she asked softly.

He never did. Why would today be different? "No, thanks." He reached for the mug, but her hand was still in the way.

Alex coughed, covering up what sounded suspiciously like a snicker.

No way. If Hailey were making a play for Tony, she was seriously desperate. She looked at him as competition, didn't she? Although the bakery ran completely opposite hours from Antonio's. Oh, plus he wasn't interested. At all.

She refilled cups around the table, and the guys dug into their prayer time.

This. This was Tony's lifeline. He listened to one man after another bare their souls before the God who loved them, coming alongside each other, holding each other up. He prayed, too, feeling the stress flit away bit by bit.

Prayer was more effective than lavender. Who knew?

All too soon, the men around the table checked their watches, emptied their mugs, and grabbed their briefcases. Dan shoved his Ranta Landscaping baseball cap over unruly curls and paused beside Tony's chair. "How you doing, man?"

"All right. You?" Tony didn't need to burden his friend down with anything the guy couldn't help with.

Dan grinned. "Everything's good. Real good."

"Excellent."

"The kids talk about you. And you'll be glad to know Mandy keeps asking her mom to make zoodles." Dan lowered his voice conspiratorially. "So far, Buddy hasn't figured out that means zucchini noodles."

"That's great." Tony rose to his feet and bumped his friend's fist.

"I know you're facing some growing pains with the restaurant." Dan searched his eyes. "Just want you to know you've made a huge difference in my family's life. I don't know what we would have done without you last winter."

"Thanks. It was my pleasure." It really had been. Dan's kids had been a mess with their mother's disappearance from their life, but they'd all found a rhythm together. Henry, the toddler, had spent many hours nestled against Tony's chest, thumb in his mouth, while Tony worked on plans for the restaurant. He missed all the kids, but the little guy, especially. "Maybe on the weekend I can come by and cook for you guys."

"Your weekend or mine?" Dan chuckled. "I wouldn't say no either way."

"My weekend is Monday and Tuesday. I might have to extend it to Wednesday this fall if I can't find more staff, though. The customers are there. Our reputation is spreading, and one of the culinary columnists did a great review a few days ago. We're hopping... and half our staff is quitting soon to go back to school."

Dan looked thoughtful. "Dixie's got experience in food service. Want me to ask her if she'd like to work for you?"

Tony squashed down the sudden hope of a reprieve, but Dixie and Dan had been married less than five months. "No. You guys need her at home."

"She's going stir crazy. Would even a couple of nights help? Or a few four-hour shifts? I can adjust my work schedule a little to get home earlier now that Linnea and Logan are back in Spokane and helping with the business."

Dan's sister had been studying horticulture design at college in Edmonds while her husband took business classes. They'd graduated last spring and moved home to help expand Ranta Landscaping.

"I appreciate the thought, Dan. I really do. But I'd hate to take Dixie away from you and the kids at all. School's started back in, so if she worked for me, she'd miss a lot of time with Mandy, and I know that kid needs her mom."

"Well, keep it in mind, and we'll do the same. Might not hurt to have a server trained who doesn't work full time and could come in if someone calls in sick or something. We're only a few blocks away."

"True that." Tony could feel himself wavering. "Thanks. Talk to her. See what she says."

Dan grinned. "I have a feeling she'll jump at the chance."

7

*Y*ou look nice." Marietta twirled her finger then winced.

Feeling self-conscious, Kenna turned in a circle. She'd gone shopping yesterday afternoon while the old woman napped and Winnie wiped down pantry shelves. Winnie had put like objects together, but hadn't alphabetized them or sorted them by size. Still, the shelves were clean, and some way-outdated items had been tossed. No one needed cream of tartar with a best-before date of 1986. Kenna had never heard of the stuff, so probably no one needed it at all. Not that she was the best judge.

"That color suits you."

Kenna refocused on her client. "Thank you." She kind of liked the pink and lavender swirls on her new tunic herself, and the gray leggings were okay, though not particularly wonderful. She'd bought several identical pairs as they'd go with everything.

All because *someone* complained of footsteps. Well, he should be happy now.

"I haven't seen Tony for a few days." Marietta's eyebrows peaked as she looked at Kenna.

"I haven't, either." Not since they'd squared off the other day. "He must be pretty busy at his restaurant."

The old lady scowled. "Too busy for his nonna?"

There was no answer for that. Kenna helped Marietta shift to the wheelchair then rolled her into the living room. "I'll make you a cup of coffee then change the sheets on your bed."

Marietta's hand on her arm stayed her. "You take good care of me. Thank you."

Startled, Kenna flashed her a glance. The temptation to say she was just doing her job faded at Marietta's expression. "You're welcome."

"Maybe I can sit on the back patio today."

Hmm. There'd be a bump getting the wheelchair over the threshold, but it should be possible to take it slowly enough. "We can try that. How about now? I can bring your coffee there."

"Could I?" Marietta tried to straighten a little in the chair but flinched.

Kenna propped the French doors open, and the warmth of early September seeped into the dining room. With it came the robust scent of tomatoes and herbs, to say nothing of the ever-present lavender. She carefully rolled the chair through and positioned it in a shady spot with a view of the flourishing garden. The blissful smile on the old lady's face when Kenna returned a few minutes later with her coffee made the effort worthwhile. "Will you be okay here while I make your bed?"

"Si."

With the bedding switched, Kenna peeked through the

window to confirm her charge was fine before shifting laundry loads and starting the sheets. She put away the previous load, tidied the laundry area, and wiped the washer and dryer with a damp cloth.

Then she headed out the back door, only to see Tony sitting in a patio chair near his grandmother. She stopped in her tracks.

Tony paused with his hand extended, holding a cardboard takeout box within inches of Marietta's knees. He looked like a kid with his hand in a cookie jar. Guilty.

"What did you bring me, Antonio?" Marietta reached a shaky hand toward the container.

"Ah, pasta primavera, Nonna." He wrenched his gaze from Kenna's. "Just the way you like it."

"You're a good boy."

Kenna crossed her arms over her chest. "I'll put that in the fridge for later."

That got everyone's attention. Marietta turned to see her, while Tony's eyebrows shot up. "Why?" he demanded. "She can have it right now if she wants. It's warm."

"It's not lunchtime for another hour."

"Who cares?"

She skewered him with a glare. "Schedules are important."

Tony opened the container, folded the lid back, and handed his grandmother a fork. He crossed his arms and raised his eyebrows at Kenna.

Kenna wavered. She'd look like an idiot grabbing the fork from an old woman, but the temptation was strong. Who was the boss here, anyway? Not him. He might be a better cook than she was — no one would ever pay good money for a meal *she* made, after all — but that didn't give him the right...

Didn't it? He was Mrs. Santoro's grandson. Why couldn't he bring her food if they both wanted? What did it hurt anyone?

Just Kenna's sense of control was at stake. She marched into the house, the quiet tennis shoes not making nearly the statement she wanted, then down the hallway and into her bedroom before shutting the door. Firmly.

Kenna slumped to sit on the edge of her bed. Was she being completely unreasonable? Tony obviously thought so, and she had let him win this round. To say nothing of him winning the round about her footwear. Why was she giving in to him? Wouldn't that make him insufferable?

He'd appeared so easygoing at first. Everyone seemed to like him, from his aunts to his cousins to the reviewers who ate at Antonio's. Was Kenna the only person who saw the irrational side of him?

Or... could it be her? She could admit to having strong opinions, a resolute sense of how things should be. But that didn't mean she had to spark off Tony Santoro like a lit match against a short fuse every time they met. It definitely wasn't the other kind of spark. He irritated her, nothing more.

He might be cute, but that didn't count for anything. He might be broad-shouldered with an athletic build, but she didn't particularly care.

Tony Santoro was nothing to her except the guy who lived downstairs and her client's seemingly favorite grandson. He was the polar opposite of Maurice Hamelin in every way imaginable, but that could only stand the entrepreneurial chef in a good light. She didn't want another man like her late husband in her life.

Wait. Stop. She didn't want another man in her life at all. Ever.

Was Tony's pasta primavera any good? It had smelled robust, savory, and delicious. And thankfully not like lavender at all.

~ ‹ ‹

"MATTEO. It is good to see you, my son." Nonna tilted her face toward Tony's dad, who dutifully kissed one cheek then the other.

Mom swooped in and did the same. "How are you, Mamma? Is Tony taking good care of you?"

As if he had the chance with Kenna around. Kenna, who stood at the entrance to the bedroom wing, arms at her sides, with a blank expression on her face. Like that was anything new. Didn't fool Tony for one red hot second. He'd met the opinionated side of the nurse far too many times.

"Please meet my nurse, Makenna Johnson."

Hamelin, Tony's brain corrected, but he managed to keep his mouth shut.

"Between her and Tony, they do well. And Winnie and Grace come often, too."

That left Aunt Genevera, who worked full-time, and Aunt Betta, who was rather timid and slightly terrified of her mother-in-law.

Kenna shot him an indiscernible look before she stepped forward with a smile to shake hands with his parents.

"My son, Matteo, and his wife, Constance. They live in Galena Landing, Idaho."

"We're here this weekend for Mamma's birthday party." Mom squeezed both Kenna's hands.

"I understand I've usurped your usual bedroom," Kenna replied. "I'm sorry."

Tony doubted that.

"Oh, that's fine. We don't mind staying with Ray and Grace this time. We're all just so thankful for the care you're providing."

All of them were thankful? Okay, fine. Tony was thankful, too. He could only wish his aunts had found someone a bit less abrasive. Some plump middle-aged nurse who didn't threaten his very existence.

He scowled at Kenna. How on earth had he allowed her to get under his skin this much? She'd been in the house for three weeks now. Aside from the odor of bland food seasoned by scorching it, she seemed to be doing a fine job.

"And how is Mamma's prognosis?" Dad shook Kenna's hand.

Nonna's eyebrows went up as she looked between them, like she wanted to know, too.

Kenna bit her lip for a second. "The healing is somewhat slower than her doctors would have liked. There's just no way to stabilize the pelvic bone completely, short of lying in the same position for weeks, and of course, that's not practical."

Nonna muttered something under her breath in Italian.

Tony was pretty sure he didn't want to know what she'd said.

"So you'll be here for a while yet?" Dad asked.

Kenna angled her head in agreement. "It looks that way.

Even the most optimistic outlook, back in August, said she'd need assistance for a minimum of two months, but it looks like three — or possibly even four — will be more realistic. We'll need to evaluate as we move forward."

Was she making that up because she needed the job? Or because she enjoyed antagonizing Tony? Nah. She wouldn't be like that. Would she?

"Well, we are certainly thankful for your help," Mom said. "Everyone has only had good things to say about you."

Kenna raised her eyebrows at him.

Great. Tony had carefully kept his opinions to himself, which made it sound like he'd been gushing along with his aunts. He certainly had not been. He just hadn't seen the point in dumping his frustration on his parents, since they lived too far away to be of any practical help. Besides, he'd told the aunts to go ahead and hire Kenna. His personal issues with her were just that. His.

Mom patted Kenna's arm, but probably didn't notice her flinch. Tony did. "Well, you just take care of Mamma this weekend and let Matt and me take care of everything else. I'll do the cooking and the cleaning and..." Mom's voice faltered as she looked around.

She was probably searching in vain for one single thing that needed tidying, dusting, or scrubbing, but she wouldn't find it.

"I can—"

"Nonsense," Mom interrupted. "I'm sure you work too hard, and we're happy to lift the burden while we're here. Take some time for yourself. Get out for a bit with your friends."

If Kenna had any friends, Tony hadn't seen or heard a peep out of them. He wasn't one to talk, though. His life revolved around the restaurant. Other than that, he lived in a vast wasteland. One crowded with his grandmother's excess belongings.

Nonna closed her eyes for a brief second.

In an instant, Kenna squatted by the wheelchair, her knit dress clinging to her perfect curves. "Would you like to lie down for a little while?"

Why did Tony keep noticing the nurse's shape? It drove him crazy. Sure, he was thankful she'd exchanged her clicking heels for soft-soled tennis shoes. The fact that she'd picked up knit dresses and leggings to go with them hadn't escaped him, either. The softer look suited her. Made her look a bit less formal. Less imposing. But that was just her outer looks and had nothing to do with her personality. *That* was just as take-charge and abrasive as before.

Tony might have barked at a young waitress last night and caused a spate of tears, but it wasn't the same thing. He ran a moderately sized business with nearly two dozen employees. He couldn't let the restaurant's reputation lapse because the girl had messed up the orders at table eighteen.

Taking care of Nonna was Kenna's job in the same way. Sure, she wasn't responsible for the range of things he was, but she was just as dedicated to making her job run smoothly. He had to hand it to her.

"Let me help you." Dad followed Kenna and the wheel-chair down the hallway.

Good luck with that, Dad.

"No. I've got it." Kenna smiled and nudged the bedroom door shut with her foot as she passed through.

Mom turned to Tony. "She seems... nice."

"I think you mean efficient."

"That, too." She smiled and looked around the living

room. "I don't think I've ever seen this place so spotless, but there appears to be some furniture missing. I guess it needed to be moved to make room for the wheelchair."

"About that." Tony glanced at the hallway as Dad paused in front of Kenna's open door then came the rest of the way with a slight frown on his face. "My aunts got a little carried away, I think. The basement storage area is so jammed full they started putting the excess in my place."

"There's almost no furniture in the guest room," Dad observed. "It's all in the basement, you say?"

"Has anyone ever noticed that Nonna has way too much stuff that she doesn't need?" Tony looked between his parents. "I don't know when someone last went through this house and decluttered it. You guys usually stay in the guest room. Did you know one of the drawers was full of Nonni's *socks*? And his clothes still hung in the closet? He's been dead since I was a kid."

Dad grimaced. "Yes, we knew that. It was always hard to find a place to put our suitcase in that room. Ray and Grace's house is much more... organized."

"We need to stage an intervention." Tony kept his voice low. "She's eighty. She could live another twenty years, and it just can't keep going like this. Having Kenna here has only brought the problem to a head."

The bedroom door clicked. Kenna skewered Tony with shooting darts. What on earth? Why would she think they shouldn't declutter? He thought she'd be the first to get on board with his plan.

"I'm a problem, am I?" Her hands rested on her shapely hips.

Uh... "That's not what I said."

_____

8

*S*he knew what she'd heard: ...*can't keep going like this. Having Kenna here has only brought the problem to a head.* So she hadn't caught the entire conversation. She hadn't needed to to get that she was a problem.

Well, fine. Kenna didn't like him, anyway. Why was it a surprise to hear Tony confirm his opinion to his parents? It wasn't. So she zipped her mouth and kept doing what she was doing, albeit with two extra people in and out of the house. Matt and Connie slept at Ray and Grace's, spent the morning with Tony, and the afternoon with Marietta.

And then it was Saturday. The family had decided on a midday party to make it easier for out-of-towners to attend. And possibly for Tony.

It was a little over two blocks to the community center. Kenna'd had to argue with Matt, but she'd won the right to push the wheelchair, a simpler solution than procuring an accessible van. Besides, Marietta seemed eager to spy on her neighbors' gardens as they made their way up the steep hill then angled over beneath the bridge.

The brick building had undergone a complete renovation several years ago. Kenna'd only heard about it because Maurice mumbled derisively about the waste of tax-payers' money in the grants the community had received for everything from a Tesla Powerwall storing energy from the rooftop solar collectors to the shiny new commercial kitchen in the back of the building, where the cooking club met. Today, Marietta's daughters-in-law bustled in and out, setting platters of sandwiches and baking on long tables.

Not cooking would be a nice change, if only for one meal. Yeah, she could soften her stance toward the chef who lived in the basement. He'd probably let her have a leftover or two from the restaurant, but there was no way she'd back down now and look a fool.

Kenna parked the wheelchair in the area decorated for the birthday girl with curving latticework, balloons, and streamers. She crouched by Marietta's side. "Are you all right? Do you need anything adjusted? May I get you a coffee or a glass of punch?" Surely the Santoro women would offer coffee the old woman liked.

Marietta patted her arm. "Thank you. I am good." She looked around her with eager eyes. "My family — they honor me."

"Yes, they do."

And they were pouring toward their matriarch like an incoming tide. Kenna retreated slightly but kept one hand on the wheelchair as a notice that she was on duty. Her one and only job was making sure her client was not overtaxed. If the situation warranted, she'd roll that wheelchair right out the door and down the sidewalk, even if they were in the middle of toasting the milestone birthday.

September sunshine streamed in through the propped-open doors and allowed free access to guests. She caught sight of Tony entering — not that she was watching for him — with a little boy perched on his shoulders. She inhaled sharply. That was a different vision of him than she'd seen before. Tony turned to the woman beside him, who had a toddler balanced on her hip. They laughed together then a man came up behind them and took the little girl. The group proceeded toward Mrs. Santoro.

Makenna straightened — not that she'd been slouching — and stared across the space at the Tesla Powerwall as though it were the most fascinating object in existence. Still, she somehow managed to follow their progress to the birthday girl.

"Happy birthday, Nonna." The woman bent and gave her grandmother a hug.

Too hard a squeeze? No, it seemed fine.

"Gina. *Grazie* for coming. Your little ones have grown."

"Ethan is five now. He just started kindergarten."

Tony lowered the child to the floor, and the little guy reached to kiss his great-grandmother's cheek. "Happy birthday, Nonna."

Marietta ran her fingers down the boy's cheek. "*Grazie*, Ethan. And your little sister is so big now."

"Emma's three!" he announced proudly.

The little girl clung to her dad's neck as the man bent to give Marietta's cheek a kiss. If anyone had mentioned the man's name, Makenna had missed it. Not that it mattered.

"Happy birthday, Nonna." Tony leaned down to kiss his grandmother. As he straightened, his gaze locked on Kenna's.

She tipped her head back just a smidge. No way would she let this kissy huggy family get to her. No way would she let the chef, handsome as he might be, past her defenses. Wait. She thought he was handsome? Whatever. She'd need to be blind not to notice his striking good looks, and she could see just fine.

"Do you need anything, Nonna?" he asked.

"Perhaps some punch."

"Got it." He waggled his eyebrows once at Kenna and strode away as the little family turned to mingle with others.

"I could have gotten that," Kenna said.

"Antonio needs to feel useful."

Right. Sure he did. He returned a moment later and pressed the glass into Marietta's hand. She drank half, and he set it down on a nearby table before standing to her other side.

Seriously? The old woman was Kenna's job, not his. He should be out there visiting with his cousins and neighbors.

A young couple came in arm-in-arm. Kenna had met Alex several times but never his girlfriend. The look of adoration on Alex's face when he squeezed her to his side sent a pang of longing through Kenna, which was ridiculous. Just as she'd told Winnie the other day, she wasn't looking for love. She'd been pretty stupid in that regard in the past, and she was going to stand on her own two feet through the rest of her life. Still, the loving look and quick kiss between the couple as they wandered amid the other guests was endearing.

Kenna didn't miss the sharp intake from her client when an elderly man with a slight build entered the center alone. Who was he? He seemed to be of Japanese descent, and he looked around with a wary expression, like the gauntlet might be too daunting to run. Just as he glanced over his shoulder and took a step backward, Alex's girlfriend hurried over to him. She took the man's arm and led him toward Mrs. Santoro.

Curiouser and curiouser.

"Marietta!" Alex's girlfriend — Marley, right? — stopped in front of the wheelchair. "Look who's come to wish you a happy birthday."

Nonna shifted gingerly and held out one hand. "Kenji. You came."

The old man bowed over her hand and kissed it.

Kenna blinked. Kenji. Who was that?

"Are you well, Marietta?" he asked.

Was the old lady blushing, or was it only the lighting? "I will be. And you?"

"Good, good." Then Kenji seemed aware of their audience. He dropped Nonna's hand and took a step backward.

"Mr. Ito!" Ray Santoro shook the man's hand and drew him away. "It's good to see you. Tell me, how did your garden do this year?"

Wasn't that just like Bridgeview? Everyone assumed everyone else had a garden... because they probably did.

Alex kissed his grandmother, drawing Kenna's attention back to her charge. "Happy birthday, Nonna." He straightened and met Kenna's gaze. "Good day, Makenna. I'd like you to meet my girlfriend, Marley Montgomery. Marley, this is Nonna's nurse, Makenna Hamelin."

The family insisted on reminding her of Maurice.

Marley smiled. "Pleased to meet you. And I'm so glad Marietta has someone living with her who can take care of her."

On the other side of the wheelchair, Tony grunted.

"I go by Johnson, actually." She shouldn't have to remind

them constantly. "Nice to meet you, Marley. You're the artist, right?"

Marley's face flushed, but she answered cheerfully. "That's me."

Alex beamed. "Have you seen her work somewhere? They have quite a collection at Bridgeview Bakery and Bistro."

"I *have* seen them. Your chickens are charming, Marley. Mrs. Santoro purchased two for her bedroom."

"Marietta." The old lady sighed.

Marley's face brightened as she crouched in front of the wheelchair. "Really? I'm so honored."

Her boyfriend shifted to the other side and chatted with Tony in low voices. They turned away from Kenna, so she couldn't overhear. Not that she was trying... much. Marley engaged the old woman in conversation for several minutes before tugging Alex away.

Kenna's hope that Tony would follow them was unfulfilled.

He measured her with his eyes — for the millionth time — then faced the next visitor.

Great. She was stuck with him.

~ ⸱ ⸱

TONY GRITTED his teeth and got through the party. If Kenna thought he was going to step aside and leave Nonna only to her care, she had another think coming. The aunts were busy hosting the party, and Tony's cousins all seemed absorbed in catching up with each other. He wouldn't mind doing that, either, but Rob and Bren had dropped by to see him this morning, and he wasn't that close with Dominic or

Basil, who'd driven out from Seattle for the weekend. Everyone else lived in town, and they could visit any time.

By two o'clock, some of the families with little kids had headed home for naps. Others had trooped across the street to the basketball courts for some three-on-three. The uncles had put away many of the tables, and the aunts chattered in the kitchen as they cleaned up from the meal.

Tony could shoot some hoops or even grab some quiet time before heading down to Antonio's for his evening shift. Instead, he took a seat at Nonna's right while her sons sat across the table, swapping stories. Times like this he missed Uncle Al. Two years had gone by since his untimely death.

"Pastor Tomas made arrangements to visit Kenji Ito one day this week," Uncle Ray announced. "What a surprise to see him here. Did you know he was coming, Mamma?"

Nonna shook her head but said nothing. Her cheeks seemed a little flushed, but it might be all the excitement.

"He's kept to himself for years," put in Uncle Franco. He grinned at his mother. "Maybe he's got a spark for you."

Nonna mumbled something in Italian. Her sons laughed. Tony raised his eyebrows at his dad across the table.

"Mamma, I noticed lots of the furniture from the house is gone. What happened to it?" Dad folded his hands on the table in front of him.

This. This was what Tony had been waiting for.

Nonna frowned. "I'm not sure."

Uncle Ray snapped his fingers. "Grace told me about that. She and the others moved things downstairs, and I was supposed to talk to you about it."

"What is to discuss?" Nonna's tone was frosty.

"It's crowded into Tony's space in the basement," Dad went on. "Mamma, I think we should have a garage sale and get rid of some of those things. There's just too much."

Nonna glared, straightened, then winced and sagged.

Tony felt just a tiny bit guilty, but not a lot. He touched Nonna's arm gently. "It is pretty crowded downstairs. One of the drawers was full of Nonni's socks."

She angled a narrowed gaze at him.

He pushed ahead. "And there really is a lot of extra furniture."

She threw up her free hand. "Fine. You take advantage of an old woman who cannot fend for herself. You take all her memories and throw them in the trash."

"That's not what we're talking about, Mamma," put in Uncle Dino. "We're talking about sorting things. Betta told me she can take a few days off this week and help."

Nonna's lips quivered, but really, this was going better than Tony had expected.

"Connie and I can stay a few days, too," said Dad. "And Winnie says she's in."

Tony leaned back in his chair, letting his gaze slide past Nonna to Kenna. Would the nurse be thrilled to facilitate some cleanup, or would it disturb her precious schedule too much? Looked like she was holding her breath as her gaze flitted over the men across the table. Then she caught Tony staring and raised her eyebrows at him.

He raised his back with a little smile. Didn't matter what she thought. She was only around for a short while. Longer than first expected, true, but she'd be gone long before Christmas. The family was going to be present all of Nonna's life and beyond. It would be a whole lot easier sorting her excess belongings while she could offer information and direction than facing the whole situation after she died. Not that he hoped she would pass away for a very long time.

Kenna's eyes softened, and her mouth twitched just a little. Was that actually a smile? Like, with humor?

He hadn't known she'd recognize an ironic situation if she tripped over it. Tony let his smile widen, just to see if her response had been his imagination. It hadn't been. Her lips definitely curved just a little.

Well. It would be nice to see eye-to-eye on something rather than feeling at loggerheads all the time. Not that they were going to be friends or anything like that. Still, not being enemies on every front would be a nice change.

9

The things Kenna did for her clients. The old woman had insisted she was well enough to attend church, even after such a big day yesterday with the birthday party. It was likely partly because she wanted to show off her visiting out-of-town family. And it was Kenna's duty to facilitate Marietta's wishes, even if it was way out of her comfort zone, so she pushed the wheelchair to the church, up the ramp, and into the bright interior.

Church wasn't really something she was familiar with. Maurice had disdained all organized religion, though he'd softened his stance in the final weeks of his life as his son Nathan sat at his bedside and told him of Jesus' love and forgiveness. Kenna had listened in from a distance, intrigued, even though the discussion hadn't been aimed at her. She didn't know whether Maurice had *accepted salvation*, as Nathan put it, but the words had certainly lingered in her mind long after the funeral. She'd finally set them aside to focus on her nursing career.

She wasn't sure she wanted to be reminded now. What

had God ever done for her? No, religion was great for some people. It seemed to work for Nathan and Jasmine and even for Maurice's youngest son, Jason, who'd been living with his older brother since their father's death. Kenna had to applaud Nathan and Jasmine for taking the troubled teen in. They'd turned Jason's life around.

"Mamma! Good to see you today." Ray Santoro bent to give his mother a kiss on the cheek before straightening to extend a smile and a hand to Kenna. "Thank you for bringing her, and welcome to Bridgeview Bible Church."

Kenna managed a smile as she shook his hand. "She wanted to come, and it's my job."

"Here let me..." He pivoted and nearly bowled Tony over.

Tony lifted the chair from the end of one row and gave Kenna a cool nod before carrying the chair into the entry.

"There you go. A good place to park." Ray pulled the wheelchair into place, beaming as though he'd performed a magic feat.

He hadn't even asked Kenna where she wanted to sit or if she needed help.

"*Grazie*, Raimondo," murmured Marietta, looking around eagerly.

Kenna sighed and edged past to the seat next to the invalid. She'd worn one of her favorite dresses today and the four-inch purple pumps that went with it, but a scan of the parade stopping to greet Marietta revealed most of the neighborhood dressed more casually. Some women even wore jeans. God allowed that? Huh.

Jasmine slid in from the other end of the row, holding baby Lillian, with Nathan then Jason and his friend Landon filling out the row. The baby grinned at Kenna, blowing a bubble from her toothless mouth and waving both fists as Jasmine said good morning.

Kenna couldn't help smiling back, even though Lillian was Maurice's granddaughter. Poor little kid was lucky to never know the man. Kenna blocked that train of thought.

A man with shoulder-length blond hair sat at the piano, his hands drifting melodiously across the keyboard as he leaned into the mic. "Good morning, friends and neighbors. Please find a seat, and let's worship our Lord together."

Marietta's well-wishers drifted away as the piano music swelled. That guy — Logan Dermott, right? — could really play. A slight movement beside Kenna drew her attention.

Marietta's free hand, the one not in a sling, turned palm-up on her lap. She sighed as she lifted her face and closed her eyes. A tear or two clung to her eyelashes.

Probably emotion, not pain, but it cut at Kenna's heart. To think she'd argued against coming today when it obviously meant so much to the old woman. A surreptitious glance around revealed many others in a similar reverent posture.

"Please stand and sing with me," invited Logan, and the congregation surged to their feet.

Not Marietta, of course. Should Kenna obey the summons or stay seated by her client? But she couldn't clearly see the screen where the lyrics appeared. She rose to her feet and watched the words, feeling as much as hearing the fervor of nearly two hundred voices lifted in song all around her.

From the corner of her eye, she'd noticed Tony slipping into a seat behind her with his visiting family. Now she could hear his fine tenor voice singing out with confidence. "I am a child of God."

After the first song, someone prayed. Then Logan led several more songs. All of them seemed to be about anxiety. About fear. Well, Kenna wasn't afraid of anything. Not much, anyway. Just that she might not get the job she wanted, since it now looked like the promotion would come up before she was free to accept it. Nothing else. She guarded herself too closely to have aspirations that could be crushed. Maurice had sucked all hope from her life.

Maybe she feared losing control of her life again.

Nah.

Well, yes, but that was okay. Vital.

But Tomas Ramirez proceeded to preach that there was no need to be anxious because God cared for people, and that He could do a better job controlling the outcome than any person could. That God had a plan for each person's life, and His goal in times of trial was to draw people closer to Him in some complicated choreography.

"'We are confident'," he read, "'that God is able to orchestrate everything to work toward something good and beautiful when we love Him and accept His invitation to live according to His plan.'"

That counted Kenna out right there. She didn't love God. How could she, when He'd never done a thing for her?

But the memory of Nathan's words to his father smote her. He'd told Maurice that God had given His Son to die for his sins. That if Maurice would only be sorry and ask forgiveness, God would acquit him and welcome him to heaven. If Nathan had told the truth, God had definitely done something for people. A big something.

Had Maurice taken up Nathan's advice?

Kenna didn't know. There was no way to tell now. Her

late husband certainly had a lot of sins, as Christians called them, which needed accounting for.

Either way, she found herself captivated by Pastor Tomas's words. It would be awesome to have someone reliable to lean on so she didn't have to carry the entire burden of her life by herself.

"Good sermon." Dad turned to Tony at the end of the service. "I always enjoy coming to church here when we're in Bridgeview for the weekend."

"I like it, too, but sometimes I miss Grace Fellowship in Arcadia Valley. They had an awesome men's group."

Dad's eyebrows rose. "I thought there was one here, too."

Tony nodded. "There is. Thursdays at six in the morning. I get why it's that time, but it's brutally early for a guy who's rarely in bed before midnight."

"I can see that." Dad leaned forward and rested his hands on Nonna's shoulders as he spoke to her.

Kenna instantly stilled, staring at Dad's hands. That woman missed nothing. She was utterly devoted to her job, to Nonna.

Which was admirable. Of course, it was. Whatever she did was perfect... except for cooking. It was downright painful to walk past the open kitchen window and smell the fumes from whatever meal had gone wrong.

Tony longed to run in there and fix everything. Prepare light, delectable meals Nonna loved. Maybe give Kenna a cooking lesson or two. How hard was it, really, not to incinerate fried eggs?

Speaking of perfect, every blond hair on her head lay precisely in its place. He'd had plenty of time during the service to analyze the long curls flowing over the shoulders of her lavender-colored dress. To notice, once again, her slim waist when she stood during worship, her sculpted calves, and those ridiculously high heels that put her almost level with him.

Not that he cared.

But he'd noticed she didn't sing, and that reminded him that she was likely not a believer, and he hadn't really been behaving like one around her. He'd been rude and antagonistic. What in that would attract her to Jesus? Nothing.

He'd pray about that. Change his attitude. Treat her with more respect, like Nonna did.

Jasmine rose to her feet next to Kenna and turned. A smirk crossed her face as she glanced between him and Kenna.

Uh... had he been staring? Not cool. Especially with his super-observant cousin around. He reached out, and Jasmine lifted the baby over. He bounced Lillian and made faces at her until she giggled.

The sound caught Kenna's attention, and she turned. An expression Tony couldn't decipher swept across her face and was gone in an instant. Whatever. He loved kids, and the best part of living back in Bridgeview was seeing his cousins' little ones in the bits of free time he had.

Dad looked over. "Are you cooking lunch for everyone, Tony?"

"Uh, sure. I can do that." His mind scrambled for what he could fix that wouldn't take long. Raiding Nonna's pantry and garden should make it pretty easy. "How many are coming?"

In his peripheral vision, Kenna stilled.

He kept his gaze from sliding to her.

Dad's hands still rested on Nonna's shoulders. "Just my generation for lunch, I think. We'll get started sorting some of the basement contents." He nodded at Jasmine. "Whoever else wants to join in can come by about mid-afternoon. I'm sure we can use all hands on deck."

Tony needed to head down to the restaurant around three, but Antonio's was closed Monday and Tuesday, so he'd have plenty of time to devote to the purge then. Meanwhile, sure, he could cook. He glanced at Kenna, frozen stock still. No time like the present to attempt amends. "Want to give me a hand in the kitchen? We can whip up something pretty quick."

She blinked, and her eyes met his. They were gray with a hint of purple. How had he not noticed that before? It didn't matter.

"Um, I could do that, I guess. If you tell me what to do."

"I'm good at that."

Jasmine snorted a laugh, and Tony turned to her. "Hazards of running a kitchen for years." Although Oriana still seemed unable to follow simple instructions.

"Sure, sure." Jasmine waved her hands. "Whatever you say. From here, it looks like you're just bossy. But it suits you. Right, Makenna?"

Kenna's perfect eyebrows rose slightly as she gave Jasmine a cool look. Good grief. Now her eyebrows were impeccable, too? Try as he might, Tony couldn't think of a thing about her that wasn't perfect, other than her cooking and her attitude toward him.

Maybe they could become friends. She'd be around for another couple of months at least, according to the doctor's report. It would be nice to have a friend rather than an enemy. He managed to crook a smile at her as he handed Lillian back to Jasmine. "We should get back home and get started then."

But Nonna's receiving line was longer than Pastor Tomas's. Everyone wanted to see her and talk to her for a minute, even though many of them had come by the community center yesterday for the birthday party.

Dad glanced between Tony and Kenna, nodding. "You kids run on ahead. I'll push Mamma home in a bit. It's not far."

Kenna eyed him. "But she's my responsibility."

"She's in good hands," Dad assured her. "I'll take care of her like she was my own mother." He winked.

Funny one, Dad.

"Okay. If it's all right with Mrs. Santoro."

Had Kenna not figured out that there were nearly a dozen Mrs. Santoros around? And Nonna preferred being called by name by the few who weren't related.

Kenna leaned over Nonna and they exchanged a whispered conversation. Nonna smiled and patted her arm before nudging her away. Guess that was the answer then.

It wasn't until Tony opened the church doors to usher Kenna out that he realized the two of them were leaving the building together as though they were a couple. They weren't, of course, no matter what it looked like. But it would be nice to not have enmity between them at the very least.

10

_A_wkward. That's all there was to it. How did she find herself walking down the sidewalk with her client's obnoxious grandson? Maybe obnoxious was too strong a word. He just seemed to have it all together and to be very settled and opinionated in his abilities. And she'd agreed to cook with him? Was she some sort of crazy? If only—

"I have an apology to make."

Kenna blinked and glanced at the man beside her. He wasn't much taller than her, at least in her current footwear, which only meant those blue eyes of his were nearly level with hers. She couldn't pretend she hadn't looked. "For what?" And why did her voice come out so breathless?

"I started right in with a chip on my shoulder the first time we met, and that wasn't fair to you. I haven't given you a fair chance with my grandmother, and you've done nothing to deserve my antagonism. I'm sorry."

Well. That was forthright. "I may have been less than easy to deal with myself. I apologize also."

Laugh lines crinkled around his eyes as his lips curled

upward just enough for his dimple to appear. "You're forgiven if I am."

Kenna bit her lip for a second. What did she have to lose? Nothing. She'd still be on guard, of course, but perhaps smoothing her bristles down would make the job easier. She nodded. "Okay."

He bumped his shoulder against hers. "Thanks. I'd like to be friends."

Wasn't that taking things a bit far? Removing active hostility was one thing. Friendship was quite something else. On the other hand, when was the last time she'd had a friend? Since long before Maurice. She'd always held everything tight, not letting anyone near. None of the nurses from her ward had checked up on her in the past month. She'd exchanged a few texts with Carol, the nurse who'd sublet the apartment, but that had been at the end of August when rent was due. Nothing had been personal.

"What are some of your hobbies?" he asked.

Kenna blinked. "I don't really have any." Unless she counted shopping. Or dusting.

"I love to read. I'll read just about anything. True crime, fantasy, old westerns. When I was a kid, I nearly always had a book in my hands. Now it's mostly ebooks. They take up less room."

No way was she admitting to reading romance novels. He'd laugh at her for sure. Besides, it took so long to get through one that reading didn't really count as a hobby.

Thankfully, they turned the corner by Marietta's house just then.

Tony opened the back gate. "I'm going to go put my Bible away and change into shorts and a T-shirt. Meet me in the garden in a few minutes?"

She looked down at her best dress. Probably a good idea for her to change, too. She'd hate to admit it, but her feet hurt just a little. It had been a few weeks since she'd worn heels all day, every day. "Okay."

Inside her room, she quickly changed into a pair of leggings and a long top before sliding her feet into casual shoes. She'd bought a pair of slip-ons. An ad claimed they were like walking on marshmallows, and the words had not just been marketing hype.

Kenna glanced at herself in the big mirror and patted her hair. She'd sprayed so much product before church that it hadn't moved a speck, but her eyes looked a little brighter than usual. Was that from the thought of having a friend? Would it become complicated because he was a guy? Because she wasn't looking for a husband or even a boyfriend. If she were, it wouldn't be a man like Tony.

She angled her head and raised her eyebrows at herself. And why not? What was wrong with him? Nothing, really. He was a Santoro, but he couldn't help that. Couldn't help Maurice hated the whole clan, but Kenna had given up caring about Maurice's opinion a long time ago. So she was going to head out there and find out what it would be like having a man for a friend. A man who could cook and wanted her help in the kitchen. Maybe she could pick up a tip or two. Heaven knew she could barely keep from burning water most days.

True to his word, he was already out in the garden when she slipped through the French doors. He looked up, grinning, as he set down a pair of large baskets. "How does eggplant parmigiana sound?"

Exotic.

Also, he had a cute smile.

Also, she didn't care. She wouldn't bother noticing his looks again. "I don't think I've ever had it."

His smile widened until his dimple appeared. "Time to remedy that. Here, grab this basket and pick the ripest tomatoes you can find in that bed over there. Some of the varieties aren't red, so you'll have to feel them for softness if you're not sure. Those vibrant yellow ones are ready, and behind that are a few Black Zebra plants. Let's aim for about half red and the other half a mix of colors."

Kenna was already in over her head, but she'd give it a whirl. "What's that you're picking?"

"The eggplants and herbs. A few onions. Jasmine and Peter will likely clear out this garden soon. I'm guessing we're due for frost. It's the middle of September, so it can't be much longer."

Kenna pressed a tomato lightly. It seemed to have some give, so hopefully it was ripe. "I don't know when we get frost."

"Yeah, me neither, especially down here close to the river. I'm sure it's a longer growing season here than where I lived in southern Idaho, but I could be wrong."

She picked another tomato, then another. "Where in southern Idaho?"

"Arcadia Valley. I cooked in my uncle's Italian restaurant in Twin Falls for the past few years."

"I thought all your uncles lived here." Except Winnie's husband was dead. *Way to put your foot in your mouth, Kenna.*

"My dad's family is here. Uncle Leo is my mom's brother."

"Did you always want to be a chef?"

Tony chuckled. "I always loved to eat. I worked as a dishwasher in a restaurant in Galena Landing when I was in high school. The head chef was a woman who took me under her wing." He rocked back on his heels, his gaze distant. "I got myself fired for impertinence, and Claire quit soon afterward. She spent that summer cooking for a forestry camp and hired me as her assistant. *That's* when I knew I wanted to be a chef. People are so appreciative of good food."

Kenna certainly was... so long as she didn't have to fix it herself. There could be a major benefit in dating a chef, let alone marrying one. Uh, not that she was interested. Best to keep that in mind.

"How about you? Did you always want to be a nurse?"

"I always wanted to have a job that offered good pay and security, and I won a scholarship. Nursing seemed like a good option, since I have an iron stomach."

"A scholarship?" Tony grinned at her. "You must be a whole lot smarter than me. I slid through high school by the skin of my teeth."

Seriously? She stared at him. "I find that hard to believe."

"Still true. I probably would have done better if I'd applied myself, but I didn't see the point. None of it interested me."

Whereas Kenna had aced her classes because they were there and because she could. It didn't much matter whether it was a science or Egyptian history. If she sat in that class, she'd be at the top of it. No wonder she'd had so few friends. All she'd done was study.

The pungent aroma of crushed herbs filled the air, bringing her back to the moment. Best to get the tomatoes picked so Tony could cook lunch for all his aunts and uncles with only a half hour's notice. And so she could watch him in action.

As a chef.

Of course, as a chef.

TONY LEANED over Kenna's shoulder and sniffed the onions and garlic as they sautéed then reached past her hip and turned down the flame. "Easy does it."

She glanced at him over her shoulder.

There was a floral scent floating lightly above the pungent alliums. Maybe he was rather close, but he didn't move. He had to keep an eye that lunch didn't burn, after all.

He'd never been tempted to keep this close of a watch over Oriana's shoulder. And it wasn't only that Kenna only knew two heat settings, high and off. Tony didn't need to flip that far in his opinion of Kenna. Just because he'd decided they needed to be friends instead of enemies didn't mean his thoughts needed to dial past simmer to boiling.

Tony backed away, but her gaze didn't release his for a long moment. The air felt cooler further from the range. Besides, he had eggplant slices waiting to be rinsed, coated, and pan-fried. He pointed at the large bowl of coarsely chopped tomatoes. "Those can go in now. Add the sprigs of herbs and give everything a good stir."

"Doesn't it need to be hotter?"

The kitchen was plenty hot. He should open the window over the sink, but it likely wouldn't help. This was crazy. "Just for a minute until it starts to bubble. Then it needs to simmer at medium-low for a bit."

Kenna glanced between him and the large pot. "Medium-low?"

What a shock she didn't know what that was. Tony couldn't help chuckling. "I'll show you when it's time."

The front door opened, and voices and laughter filtered through the house. Dad. Uncle Ray. Aunt Genevera. Having that entire generation over to Nonna's for Sunday lunch upset the entire fabric of the Santoro clan. Normally, all his cousins went to their parents' houses after church, while he and Nonna rotated between the families.

Tony rinsed the sliced eggplant, keeping an eye as Kenna transferred the tomatoes to the large pot.

"Anything I can do to help?" Aunt Winnie stood in the doorway. "I baked French bread yesterday and brought over a couple of loaves. I took a chance it might go with whatever you're making. May I add it smells fabulous in here? What's cooking?"

"Eggplant parmigiana. And I think garlic toast would go very well with it. Thanks, Aunt Winnie." Tony reached for a container of bread crumbs and dumped some in a bowl.

"Want me to prep it?"

Why was he even hesitating? He liked Aunt Winnie. No doubt a gathering of her late husband's family reminded her once again of what she'd lost. But he'd kind of enjoyed the brief time he and Kenna had worked together, just the two of them. Which was all kinds of silly.

"Sure. Plenty of room on the far side, and I know Nonna has several more cookie sheets." He gestured at his own assembly line on the island. "I'm using most of them for the eggplant at the moment. I'll need the top oven soon, but you can use the bottom oven when you're ready..."

Winnie set the bread on the counter and stood beside Kenna. "Mmm. That smells good."

Kenna shifted away slightly, offering an awkward smile to Winnie. "I'm just following directions."

Huh. It wasn't just him she had trouble relating to. Tony sifted through what little he'd figured out about her. A loner. Burned somehow, maybe even before Maurice Hamelin. He'd never met the man, but he'd heard plenty of stories about the alcoholic who'd pretty much drank himself to death.

Tony set his pot of oil on the other front burner and let it heat while he dredged the eggplant slices.

Pungent garlic filled the air as Aunt Winnie crushed several cloves.

Kenna stirred the tomato sauce and glanced over at Winnie with a slight frown. "Don't you people know garlic powder has been invented?"

Tony chuckled. "I've heard of it."

She turned her gray eyes on him. "Then why...?"

"The real thing has way more flavor, plus the nutrients are still intact. Trust me, it kicks things up a notch. Just like using the fresh herbs in the tomato sauce instead of dried ones that might have been in the cupboard ten years."

"But what about in winter? You can't just go pick those things all year, can you?"

"The basil and thyme? No, not in this climate. We'll chop and freeze most of it in oil for winter use."

"I don't get it."

He glanced at her. Again, so close. He lowered a slice of eggplant into the hot oil and adjusted the knob a smidge. "Every little decision makes a difference to the overall quality. A good example is a vine-ripened tomato over one picked before its prime and ripened with gas. That's what you get in most supermarkets."

Kenna nodded slowly.

"Then when you add fresh onions and garlic and herbs from the backyard, every ingredient is at its freshest and most nutritious. It all adds up to heightened flavor, and it's better for your body."

"Do you do all that in the restaurant? Because you serve, what, hundreds of people a night? You can't possibly—"

"I do. Yes, it's a challenge, especially sourcing. Peter and Jasmine have so many clients for Bridgeview Backyards they can't supply Antonio's as well. Their business just isn't big enough. But I've been working hard on my own supply chain, right down to growing herbs and greens on the rooftop patio all summer."

Kenna studied him.

He tore his gaze away to fish out the eggplant and add more slices to the hot oil. "It's like anything in life," he said slowly.

"Hmm?"

"Choices add up, whether good ones or bad ones."

She turned away abruptly. "They sure do."

*K*enna kept an eye on Marietta throughout the meal. The old woman was quiet compared to the otherwise boisterous group. As Tony and Winnie began clearing the table, Kenna leaned closer. "Ready to lie down a bit?"

Marietta sent her a sharp look. "While they throw away my memories? No."

Ray patted his mother's hand. "Today we are sorting only. You will have final say."

Bad idea. Marietta's *final say* had resulted in keeping the socks of a man dead twenty-five years.

"I *am* weary."

Kenna knew her cue when she heard it. She rose, folded her napkin, and laid it down. "Then let's go. It's time to take your pain medication, anyway." She glanced around the table, snagging for a second on Tony's sympathetic smile. At least he knew better than to offer help with his grandmother.

By the time she had Marietta settled and returned, only

Tony was in the kitchen, slotting plates into the dishwasher. "Where is everyone?"

"Downstairs in the storage room." He offered a lopsided grin. "Jasmine and Fran came over, too, but I need to head down to the restaurant soon, so I figured I'd clean up from lunch and leave my family to it."

"Cleaning up is my job."

"I made the mess."

Kenna crossed her arms over her chest. "I suppose you are the chef *and* the dishwasher *and* the janitor at Antonio's?"

The laugh lines crinkled around his eyes again.

She melted a little when they did that.

"No, you're right. I have employees for those things. But it's different at home."

"Only if you live alone." Or had a spouse like Maurice, who believed it was all women's work. The yard had been, too, for that matter.

Kenna crossed over to the sink, peeking into the tomato sauce pot as she passed the stove. Tony had already put the leftovers away. She turned on the faucet and added a squirt of dish soap.

He shook his head. "You don't have to. It's okay to relax and let someone else step up for a bit."

She raised her eyebrows at him. "Says the man who's still got a full day's work to do. If anyone should be taking a quick break, it would be you."

Tony chuckled and glanced at the clock. "Too late for that." He added a detergent tablet to the dispenser, snapped the door shut, and pressed the *start* button. "But I won't kick you out of the kitchen. This time."

She deserved that for how rude she'd been to him in

the early days. Besides, maybe the work would be more fun with a friend. They'd agreed on a new relationship, right?

"How's Nonna really doing?" Tony dipped a cloth in the sudsy water and wrung it out before starting to wipe the counter.

"There's a lot going on this weekend." Kenna slipped one of the baking sheets into the sink, washed it, and set it in the drain rack. "But I think she's okay."

"Good. I appreciate you won't let her overdo herself."

"She was already asleep by the time I'd drawn her curtains."

Tony swished his cloth in the sink, bumping into her hand. Startled, she pulled away, and water sloshed over the edge.

"Sorry." He even sounded contrite.

"It's fine. Just surprised me." It wasn't fine, though. Only yesterday, she'd held the line and kept any emotional response to this man at bay. Something else seemed to have slipped through when she cracked the door open to friendship, but there was no need at all to react to an innocent brush and start fantasizing about more. She was done with relationships, remember?

Tony shifted out of her zone and wiped the kitchen island.

With a deep, shaky breath, she washed another baking sheet then the next, completely aware of where he was, even when he moved over to the table. This was ridiculous. He couldn't leave for the restaurant quickly enough to suit her. She needed to find her equilibrium and hold on until this crazy consciousness cooled off.

This time when he returned to rinse his cloth, she

stepped aside, but he was still close enough for his after-shave to tease her nostrils.

"Have you been down to Antonio's for dinner yet? You should come sometime."

Sure. Because a high-end restaurant was the perfect place for someone dining alone. Dream come true. Some-how, she managed to stifle the eye-roll. "I eat with your grandmother."

He turned to look at her from mere inches away. "Don't you get any days off?"

Kenna shrugged. "There's no need. I have nowhere to go."

That lopsided grin. "Except Antonio's."

Tony really was a good cook. Far better than she was, not that everything was about competition. But seeing him in action today aroused her curiosity about his restaurant. Still... eating alone in a fancy place? But she had no one to invite.

"Tell you what." He scanned her face. "I'll ask Aunt Grace if she can spare an hour or two on Wednesday or Thursday evening, maybe around nine o'clock when it's slowed down a bit. Then I can invite you right into the kitchen. There's a staff table where you'd be out of the way but still close to the action. How does that sound?"

Kenna opened her mouth and closed it again. It sounded awesome. Special.

Like a date.

Except a date with a man who wasn't there. So that was just weird. Besides, they were friends, nothing more. It had been so long since she'd had a real friend, let alone a guy friend, that she didn't even know how to handle it.

On the flip side, if a woman invited her, she wouldn't

read anything into it. Tony was just proving the friendship he'd extended earlier. "That sounds nice. If it doesn't put her out too much."

He grinned. "Uncle Ray's a pilot, and all their kids are grown. When he's out of town, I'm sure she wouldn't mind. I'll check on their schedule."

"Okay."

Tony's smile widened enough to activate the dimple beside his full lips.

She jerked her gaze away. Nothing good could come of thoughts like those. She'd get used to having a friend, and then her hormones would settle down, and everything would be good.

Although the fluttering emotions were a little on the tantalizing side in the meanwhile.

༄ ༅ ༆

ALL DAY MONDAY AND TUESDAY, Tony worked alongside his extended family unearthing treasures from Nonna's storage room. Uncle Dino quietly disposed of the black socks and ratty white undershirts. Aunt Gen confirmed that a local animal shelter would be happy for boxes of threadbare towels. The plastic grocery bag full of empty prescription bottles was added to the stack of recycling.

Kenna wandered downstairs during Nonna's nap and looked over Tony's shoulder as he opened a drawer in yet another old dresser. "What's that?"

"Good question." He lifted a lacquer box out, black and red in a diagonal pattern, inlaid with birds and flowers in what looked like gold leaf. "This doesn't look Italian at all."

"More like Japanese."

He studied Kenna. She was so close. "My thoughts exactly." He tipped the lid open. A children's Valentine lay inside. "Huh." He picked up the cut-out of a boy with a fishing pole and turned it over.

To: Marietta

From: Kenji

Tony blinked. Kenji? Kenji Ito? Could there be another?

"There's more." Kenna's voice was low.

Three more Valentines lay inside the little box, all bearing the same inscription.

"Uh, Dad? Uncle Ray?" Tony laid the small cards in their nest and closed the lid. "Here's something you need to see."

Dad set down the box he'd held and angled a curious glance their direction. "What's that?"

Tony held out the lacquer box. "Why don't you tell me?"

"Looks Japanese." Dad turned the box over in his hands as his brothers crowded close.

"Nice work." Uncle Franco slid a thick finger across the lid. "Good joinery."

Dad tipped open the inlaid lid. "What's this?"

Uncle Dino turned the top Valentine over. "To Marietta. From Kenji?" His voice rose in surprise along with his eyebrows.

"How old was Mamma when she married Papa?" Dad turned to his eldest brother.

"Not quite seventeen." Ray frowned slightly and lifted out another Valentine. "I remember Kenji from when I was a boy. He and Papa were friends. I never dreamed Mamma had a thing for Kenji."

"Didn't children exchange Valentines with everyone in their class back then?" asked Aunt Grace.

"I'm sure they did," Uncle Dino said slowly. "But it looks

like he gave her this box, too. And only his Valentines are inside it."

Uncle Franco pursed his lips. "Which makes it more significant. Huh. Who knew?"

Uncle Ray chuckled, shaking his head. "I certainly never guessed. As far as I know, our parents loved each other truly and deeply all the years they had together."

"Kenji's wife passed away, what, ten years ago?" asked Aunt Genevera.

Uncle Franco nodded at his wife. "About that, yes. They had no children. He's kept very much to himself all these years... until Mamma's birthday party."

"You think he still carries a flame for her?" Dad asked. "I'm honestly not too sure how I feel about that thought."

Tony got that. He felt the same way. Confused, and a bit like he'd stumbled across something Nonna had preferred to keep hidden.

Aunt Gen stepped closer and ran her finger across the inlaid box. "It's obviously something we can't get rid of without showing her. Definitely not in the same category as suspenders that lost their snap decades ago."

The brothers looked at each other.

Tony wouldn't half mind being a fly on the wall to eavesdrop on the upcoming conversation.

Dad poked his chin toward Tony. "Is there anything else we should know first?"

Kenna's hand reached past Tony and lifted a package wrapped in red silk cloth.

Why hadn't he seen that? He'd been so fixated on the lacquer box he hadn't looked any further. But now the drawer was empty. He watched as Kenna handed the object to Uncle Ray.

Time froze. Not even a whisper sounded in the basement room, illuminated with only a few naked light bulbs in
the ceiling, scented with mothballs and dust.

Uncle Ray unfolded the cloth, beautiful in its own right,
a vibrant red with gold embossing thread forming plum
blossoms. His wife rescued the silk as a black journal came
into view. He opened the cover and lifted out a photo of a
pair of teenagers. One, a Japanese boy; the other, a brown-
haired girl laughing up at him.

Aunt Grace took the photo and passed it around. Uncle
Ray closed the journal.

Silence settled on the room with a thick, stifling cover
as the family looked between each other and the objects.

Tony barely dared breathe. It felt as though a thread had
been pulled out of his own life and, with every exhale, the
fabric unraveled further. But that wasn't true. These were
still his uncles and aunts. Nonna had loved her husband. He
knew that, even though he had no personal memories of the
man he'd called Nonni.

"Now?" asked Uncle Ray at last. "Or later?"

"We might find more." Aunt Gen reached for the journal, but Uncle Ray shook his head and didn't relinquish it.

"We've found enough." Uncle Franco's voice was heavy.
"It must be now."

"No." Kenna shifted closer to the door, blocking it. "Sh-
she's asleep. Please don't wake her for this."

The thought of his grandmother suffering a heart attack
at the shock of this resurfacing memory made Tony cringe.
Definitely best not to thrust the evidence beneath her nose
before she'd fully woken up.

Uncle Dino looked sharply at Kenna. "Don't you worry,
coming so far while she sleeps?"

Kenna lifted her phone from a deep pocket. "We have a monitor app. She'll call my name when she wakens."

He nodded. "Tony, put these things by the door. We'll take them up later when we go. I only pray we find nothing to add to the evidence."

Tony tucked the items into a small cardboard box, carried it through to his part of the basement, and set it on the counter. He braced his hands on the edge and stared out the high window, his mind whirling.

He'd never thought of what life must have been like for his grandparents as young people. Nonna had crossed the Atlantic as a young girl after the war, with her parents and sister. Nonni's family had already lived in Spokane a generation, his father a supervisor in one of the area's aluminum plants.

But to think of Nonna as a young girl interested in a different boy... that was just too strange. Too off-putting.

He only became aware of Kenna beside him by her floral fragrance. "You snuck up on me."

She laughed and arched her eyebrows. "These are quiet, sneaky shoes."

"About that. I'm sorry." Although he had to admit he liked the softer look on her. "I was a jerk."

"Me, too." She sighed. "I never thought about anyone but myself."

Tony had a thousand questions at that comment, but zipped them inside. "I'm glad we're friends now."

"Me, too." She stared out the window. Her cheeks seemed a bit pinker than usual. Probably a bit more makeup. Her lips seemed pinker, too.

He bumped her shoulder with his own, just enough to

make contact. Just enough to see if he might be imagining things.

Kenna met his gaze, her gray eyes wide, her lips slightly parted. She was only a few inches away.

Tony pressed a little closer.

So did she.

He pulled away. What was he, some kind of crazy? He was in no position to start a relationship with anyone, let alone his grandmother's nurse. He didn't even have his own place to live. This situation had *temporary* stamped all over it. He didn't need a temporary relationship to round it out.

12

*I*f Tony hadn't pulled away, she would have. Absolutely.

Kenna jogged up the outside steps from the basement apartment — an exercise much easier in her new slip-ons than her heels — and entered the house via the patio doors. She tilted her head a moment. Whew. It was still quiet. She didn't want to face Mrs. Santoro right now. Not after the discovery of the old woman's mementoes... or the discovery that Tony might mean something to Kenna.

Or might not. Just because he'd called an end to hostilities and invited her to Antonio's did not mean anything further. In no way did she *want* anything more. She was done with men, remember? Completely, undeniably, and forever.

She dug into the bottom drawer of her dresser, underneath the four pairs of identical gray leggings, and pulled out a framed photo of her wedding to Maurice in Vegas. She propped it on top of the dresser and stared at it.

There. Seeing that every day would help keep her from

doing something foolish again. One idiot action in a lifetime was enough.

Kenna took a long cleansing breath before her gaze landed on the church bulletin from Sunday. The pastor had spoken of setting aside anxiety and leaning into peace. How did someone do that? She picked up the paper and opened it.

Don't be anxious about things; instead, pray. Pray about everything. He longs to hear your requests, so talk to God about your needs and be thankful for what has come. And know that the peace of God (a peace that is beyond any and all of our human understanding) will stand watch over your hearts and minds in Jesus, the Anointed One. Philippians 4:6-7 (The Voice)

The knot in her gut said she was anxious, no matter how much she denied it. But praying wasn't a medically acceptable answer. Meditation for light cases. Counseling, maybe, or hypnosis for deeper problems.

Been there, done that. And it hadn't helped.

That wasn't entirely true. It had brought her to a place where she could cope, so long as she could control her environment. If she couldn't, things unraveled quickly.

A rustling sound caught her attention from her phone. Mrs. Santoro was awake.

Kenna hesitated a moment and gave her wedding photo a salute. She'd remember.

"Kenna?" called Marietta.

"I'm right here." She hurried across the hall and nudged the door open. "Did you have a good sleep?" She rounded the bed then swept the curtains aside, welcoming in the mid-afternoon sunshine.

"Si." The old woman strained to raise herself on her

good elbow. "The pain in my side, it is not so much these days."

"I'm glad to hear that. The doctors did say the ribs would likely be the first to heal. Then your arm."

"It takes so long."

"I know." Kenna brought the wheelchair into position and set the brakes. "Would you like to have biscotti with your coffee? Genevera brought some."

Marietta scowled. "Where are my sons?"

"Um... downstairs."

"Meddling."

Hard to deny, with today's finds. Kenna helped Marietta to the chair then wheeled her down the hallway. "Would you like to sit in the living room or on the patio?"

"Outside. Soon it will be too cold. I have missed half the summer."

The complaining was not typical. Kenna eased the wheels over the threshold and returned to the kitchen to operate the pressurized moka coffeemaker. The results were a little stronger than she could stomach herself, to say nothing of it being too late in the day for caffeine. She fixed herself a chamomile tea and took a tray out to the patio.

"The bees are busy in the lavender." Marietta pointed a shaky finger, sounding a bit less grumpy.

"Jasmine's bees, right? From the hives in the community garden next door?" Kenna inhaled the sun-warmed sweetness of the spiky blooms amid the drone of a few buzzing bees.

Marietta nodded. "She has already harvested the honey."

Which Kenna knew, since Jasmine had brought several jars of liquid gold over last week. The flavor was something Kenna had never tasted before, and dollops of honey were finding themselves into teacups that previously would have been consumed unsweetened.

The basement door creaked, and heavy footsteps mounted the concrete steps. Men's voices murmured.

Kenna's heart seized. She might be curious, but she wasn't part of the Santoro family and shouldn't intrude on this moment. Nor did she want to see Tony until she'd submerged those unwanted feelings. Mentally, she grabbed onto an image of Maurice. She'd use that as a shield.

"Mamma? I trust you had a good nap." Ray leaned over his mother and gave her a kiss on each cheek.

She nodded and accepted the same from her other three sons. Then she looked down as her hands twisted in her lap.

Was she thinking of the son who'd passed on, or had she caught an undertone in the men's greetings?

Kenna rose. "May I put on a pot of coffee for everyone? It won't take long."

Dino shook his head. "Betta and I need to leave in just a few minutes. We've got little Gavin this evening while Dafne works."

Marietta's daughters-in-law took seats near their husbands. From the corner of her eye, Kenna noticed Tony standing back where his grandmother couldn't see him.

Ray produced the cardboard box from behind his back and set it on the patio stones in front of him. "Mamma, we did find something today that brought some questions."

The old woman's head tilted up just enough to catch sight of the box. She frowned as though seeking the associated memory then her face paled as Ray drew out the lacquer box.

"It looks like you and Kenji Ito have known each other a very long time," Ray observed.

Marietta's free hand pressed over her mouth.

"It's a beautiful box, Mamma. Did Kenji make it?"

She shook her head, a tiny but vehement shake.

"It's okay, Mamma. We aren't angry. This happened before you married Papa, right? You were just a girl. The journal—"

Her gaze flew to his face, and the blood rushed back to her cheeks as she held out a hand as though to stop him.

"We didn't read it. It's yours."

Franco cleared his throat. "We saw the photo of the two of you, though."

"And the Valentines," added Matt, Tony's dad.

"You can tell us all about it if you like," said Dino. "Or not. Your choice." He reached for Betta's hand. "We must go now, so if there is a tale, save it for another time, per favore."

"We'll go, too." Franco rose to his feet. "It is no big thing. Genevera fell in love with five men before she met me. It means nothing to us now."

That was gracious of him.

The others all stood as one. Matt leaned over his mother and kissed her cheek. "We'll be back later, Mamma. Take care." He gave Kenna a significant look.

She read it loud and clear. *Make sure she's all right.* Like the old lady could be after a shock like this one. The Santoro men and their wives filed around the house.

Only then did Tony come forward and crouch at his grandmother's side. "Are you okay, Nonna?"

Marietta pointed a quivering finger toward the box a few feet away. "Per favore?"

"Sure, Nonna." Tony set the lacquer box on her lap then laid the silk-wrapped journal on the little table beside her coffee cup. He glanced at Kenna, but she didn't meet his gaze. On silent feet, he rounded the corner of the house.

Leaving Kenna with a woman who'd just endured a major shock. She didn't want to be here, but Marietta was her responsibility. She hadn't needed Matt's imploring look to know that.

TONY WANDERED the two blocks down to the riverfront path. He was tempted to go into Antonio's. Cook up a big plate of comfort food, but who was there to share it with? No one. Nor did he need to stuff his face with carbs and cheese, much as the thought tantalized.

Wade Roper waved to him from the food forest near the river. "Hi there!"

"Hey, Wade." Tony didn't feel like talking, but Wade backed down a ladder leaning against an apple tree.

"Tuesday must be your day off."

"It is. We're open Wednesday through Sunday evenings."

Wade tossed him an apple, which Tony caught reflex-ively. "Always looks busy over there." He poked his chin in the direction of the restaurant then took a big bite of a juicy apple.

Tony nodded and did the same. The crisp sweetness neutralized the sourness in his mouth. He held up the fruit. "Thanks."

"There's lots there. Help yourself any time. That's what the project is for."

"This must keep you pretty busy." Tony hadn't taken the time to have a good look around before, but there were a couple of dozen trees in different species of fruits and nuts as well as a row of brambles creating a hedge on two sides of the lot.

Wade ran his hand through his hair then resettled his *Fish and Wildlife* ball cap on his head. "The beauty is it mostly runs itself, honestly. Sustainability and self-efficiency is the name of the game in permaculture. Once more of the fruiting varieties mature, there'll be more work picking, but since it's a free community resource, I think the labor will spread itself out."

"Looks like Jasmine's part of your plan." Tony pointed to a pair of beehives.

Wade chuckled. "She's been an enthusiastic supporter since the beginning, for sure. She's pretty busy now with the baby and Bridgeview Backyards, but at least I have the benefit of handy pollinators to entice her back from time to time."

Tony grinned. "I'm sure they do."

"How's your grandmother feeling?"

Talk about a smile-fader. "Better. You and Rebekah were at her birthday party on Saturday, weren't you?"

Wade nodded. "I wasn't sure if she was hepped up on painkillers or really doing as well as she looked."

"Probably the painkillers. The actual healing is slower than doctors expected, but it's coming."

"Gotta be hard when you're eighty."

"Yeah."

"Nice she's got a live-in nurse, though. Big load off the family."

And a big load *on* Tony. Then add Kenji Ito. "Yes, Kenna makes all the difference. There was a brief discussion on whether Nonna would live with one of her sons during her convalescence, but she's pretty set in her ways and wanted to stay at home. I can't say I blame her."

"Pretty nurse."

Was the man fishing? He'd get nowhere. "Sure. Good credentials, too." Tony could clamp down the lid of Wade's curiosity by telling him how much Kenna hated him and booted him out of Nonna's kitchen, but that was ancient history, and he didn't really want to drag her name through the mud just because he was currently confused about his feelings. The feelings he didn't have.

Wade nodded and munched another bite of his apple.

Down the block, Dan and Dixie pulled into their driveway. Tony pointed. "I need to talk to Dan. Nice running into you."

"Sure, man. Come pick a basket of apples any time you like."

"Enough for a crostata for a special dessert menu one night?"

"I don't see why not. Help yourself."

"Thanks. I appreciate it." Tony waved and crossed the street.

Dan's son Henry saw him, dodged his dad, and barreled down the sidewalk as fast as his toddler legs would churn.

"Hey, little guy." Tony scooped the two-year-old onto his shoulders.

"Nice catch," yelled Dixie. "He's quick."

Henry dug his fingers into Tony's hair, holding tight as he bounced with glee.

Tony loved this boy. Living with Dan and the three kids last winter had piqued his enjoyment of reading stories, playing cars, and making kid-friendly meals. He'd even managed to get picky Buddy eating vegetables.

And now? The desire to have kids of his own roared back over him. He'd missed these three. He missed Gina's kids. Jasmine's baby was great, but she wasn't enough. He wanted his own.

Did Kenna want kids?

And did it matter whether she did or not?

13

*T*he old lady stared out the living room into a gray, foggy morning, a slight frown marring her lined face.

The weather did the same thing to Kenna, but it wasn't only that. It was concern for her client.

Marietta hadn't spoken of Kenji Ito since her sons had brought the mementoes to her several days ago. She'd seemed pensive — melancholy, even — ever since, and the items lay on her bedside table right next to a photo of a middle-aged couple that must be Marietta and her late husband.

Should Kenna ask her client about it? Maybe it would be easier since she wasn't family. Maybe it would help Marietta sort out her feelings. It was obvious she was conflicted.

Not that Kenna knew anything about dealing with stress in a healthy way. If she had, she'd have walked out on Maurice years before he passed away. Better yet, she'd have been wiser to begin with and never taken that fateful trip to Las Vegas with him.

Too late for all that now, but at least she was free of the man.

Did Marietta feel the same about her husband? That he'd been a mistake, and she should have married Kenji instead?

Kenna couldn't imagine it. Not with the fondness with which the old lady spoke of Salvador and her obvious love for her sons and grandchildren. She'd seemed at peace, even amid the pain, before the revelation the other day.

"You have heavy thoughts."

Kenna swung her gaze toward Marietta, whose sharp eyes focused on her. She forced a smile. "Gray thoughts for a gray day."

"Into each life some rain must fall."

"That sounds... profound."

"It is from a poem by Henry Wadsworth Longfellow, 'The Rainy Day.' Do you know it?"

The poet's name sounded vaguely familiar, but Kenna couldn't place it. She shook her head.

"Longfellow laments the days that are dark and dreary but concludes his ballad with the famous words: *Be still, sad heart, and cease repining. Behind the clouds is the sun still shining; thy fate is the common fate of all. Into each life some rain must fall; some days must be dark and dreary.*"

Kenna turned the words over in her mind. They made a sort of sense. Rain and sunshine. Sadness and joy. Yes, that sounded like life, a constant rollercoaster of bad and good. Mostly bad for her, but maybe not for everyone.

She didn't like the fluctuation. Wouldn't it be better if life were on an even keel and didn't vary so much? Still, then she'd miss the times of great joy. Kenna nearly snorted. She'd had so few of those, but she was only thirty-three, maybe a third of the way through her days. Was it possible there was joy to come?

A quick vision of Tony flickered in her mind, but she banished it. Friends was one thing. More was something else, and highly unlikely.

"We must accept the bad with the good." The old lady was back to staring out the window. "When there are dark and stormy times, we must hold fast to a loving God. He is faithful and will never let us go."

Kenna shook her head, as though the action would dislodge the tears that suddenly clung to her eyelashes.

"To cling to our God, we must know Him. Love Him as He loves us. Do you know Him, Makenna?"

"Not really. He's never been part of my life."

"But He has." Marietta's voice gentled. "He has guided your steps your whole life long. He has waited for you to turn to Him."

"If He guided me, I would never have married Maurice." Kenna clapped her hand over her mouth. Her doubts and pain were never to be spoken aloud. Never.

"And yet God was still with you. We all make mistakes."

"Was marrying Salvador a mistake?" Oh, man. How were these words escaping her mouth? This was none of her business, and not an improvement over talking about Maurice.

"Salvador? Never a mistake. He was a wonderful man. A man who walked with God and loved his wife and family fiercely. He was taken much too soon. How he would have loved to see his grandchildren grow up, to meet his great-grandchildren."

"But... Kenji..."

Marietta shook her head, a soft smile gracing her lips. "Kenji and I were never meant to be. He was a fine boy, the love of a young girl. But when Salvador came into my life, he swept me off my feet, and there was no looking back." Although the faraway look in her eyes belied the words.

"But now?" Kenna held her breath.

"There is nothing but fondness for an old friend. I am eighty years old, Makenna. Kenji is eighty-six."

"That's not too old." Who was Kenna kidding? She lived like thirty-three was too old.

"My body is broken. My ways are set. My family is around me. No, there is nothing more for me. I am content."

Kenna's protest died on her lips. It certainly wasn't her place to push her client toward a new relationship at her age.

"Kenji's wife was a lovely Japanese woman. Fumiko was her name, and she was very suited to Kenji. Her family, like his, had been relocated to Spokane during the war. They shared many experiences and traditions."

Kenna had heard of the internment camps, of course. How the American government had forced the Japanese away from coastal areas under the suspicion that their allegiance still lay with their homeland, currently at war with the USA. Homes and businesses had been confiscated, and the good names of American citizens clouded with racism and fear. The reminder shed a new light on the young love between a Japanese boy and an Italian girl. Although, hadn't Italy also been seen as an enemy?

Too confusing. She studied the older woman through new eyes. Marietta had lived through events that had since become footnotes in dusty history books.

"Through all those circumstances," Marietta mused, "God has been faithful to those who follow Him. It says in the book of Romans, 'We know that in all things God works for the good of those who love him, who have been called according to his purpose.'"

"Called?" Kenna raised her eyebrows. If anyone was calling her, she sure hadn't heard.

"In Second Peter 3:9, it says, 'The Lord is not slow in keeping his promise, as some understand slowness. Instead he is patient with you, not wanting anyone to perish, but everyone to come to repentance.'"

If the old lady thought she was clarifying things, she was dead wrong. But there were a few words there in the middle about not wanting anyone to perish. Was that the same as being called?

"Jesus died for you, Makenna Johnson Hamelin. He did it because He loves you and has called you to His purpose. He is patiently waiting for you to come to Him in repentance, because He doesn't want you to perish."

That brought the situation into clearer focus. Unsteadily, Kenna rose to her feet. "May I fix you a cup of coffee?" Because she needed this conversation to be over. Now.

DIXIE DROPPED DRAMATICALLY onto the bench surrounding the table at the back of the kitchen in Antonio's. "Well, that was excitement I never need to see again."

Tony glanced at the clock as he plated a vegetarian lasagna. Yep, time for her break. "What happened?"

"The guy at table twenty-two choked on a piece of sausage, and the guy from twenty-four gave him the Heimlich, and then there was a big argument about whether the

Heimlich was even the right thing to do. Apparently, it's outdated. Who knew?"

Tony set the plate on the shelf and pulled a heat lamp down before tapping the bell. "Twelve up!" Then he glanced at the next order before turning back to the scramble on his grill.

"Is the guy okay?"

"Yeah, he's fine."

"I should get a first aid course for all employees."

"Might not be a bad idea. I had no idea what to do. It all happened so fast, just like a few weeks ago when Henry choked on his sandwich. I just stared, frozen, while Dan grabbed him and gave him a few whacks on the back. The piece of bread flew out of his mouth, and he started to cry, and it was awful. But he's okay, too."

Definitely needed a first aid course around here. "I should go out and talk to the couple. That was the stuffed peppers and the baked ziti, right?"

Dixie waved her hand. "They've left already."

Tony frowned. "I should know these things as soon as they happen, so I can give my personal apologies and make sure our reputation doesn't suffer. What if he was a culinary critic? Or someone watching was?"

"I never thought of that. They left a good tip, though."

Whew on the tip. Still, the kinds of establishments where Dixie had gained her food service experience were big on skimpy clothes and the ability to flirt, not the kinds of places where a positive reputation meant anything.

It meant a lot to Tony. A few critical reviews in the Spokesman-Review and he'd be running a second-class restaurant with little hope of paying his uncles back for their deep investment into Antonio's. They weren't holding their hands out, but that didn't keep Tony from feeling the pressure. It was all on him.

An award from the Culinary Arts Guild at their annual banquet would go a long way to cementing Antonio's as an esteemed restaurant.

Having someone choke to death on a bite of sausage would have the opposite effect.

Tony slid a plate in front of Dixie then returned to the orders still trickling in from the dining room.

"We're almost out of kale and eggplant," announced Oriana.

Eight o'clock, and they were open until ten-thirty. Great. "How close to out?" His mind raced. Was there anywhere he could score a late-night delivery? And where could he find more before tomorrow's shift began? There'd be no rest for the weary, apparently.

Oriana tilted the remaining produce bins toward him.

Tony nodded. They might squeak through. If they had to pull one of the specials later, then they would.

"Hey, I saw your grandmother in church last Sunday. How's she doing?" Dixie forked a bite of pasta into her mouth.

"She's healing a bit slower than we hoped." He chopped a steak while Oriana plated a salad. "But she's improving, and that's what counts."

"So that nurse will still be there for a while?"

Tony glanced over at Dixie. Figured Dixie wouldn't be a fan of Kenna's. Not too long ago, he hadn't been, either. "Kenna? Another couple of months, sounds like."

"I don't know how you stand having her around."

Oriana looked between them, curiosity shining from her

eyes. At Tony's raised eyebrows, she flushed and turned to strain the pasta.

One of the negatives of having hired wait staff he knew personally. Dixie said what she thought all the time. No pretense there.

"Kenna's really good with Nonna. That's the important thing. She's an excellent nurse."

"Huh. Dan said—"

Tony quelled her with a look. What he said in men's prayer breakfast on a Thursday morning should not come back to haunt him in his restaurant kitchen.

"Sorry." Dixie glanced at the clock and buckled down to her meal. At the end of her break, she came close to Tony. "Sorry for talking out of turn," she said quietly as Oriana headed into the walk-in cooler for another bin of greens.

"Just be careful, please." Tony hated to come down hard on Dixie, but boundaries were beautiful things. "And seriously, Kenna's fine. Nonna is in expert care, and that's a relief to the whole family."

"That's good then." Dixie didn't sound convinced, but that didn't matter. "I'll go finish out my shift. Just don't go falling for someone who's just *fine*, buddy. And I don't think she's a Christian."

The cooler door slammed shut as Oriana reentered the cooking area. Dixie waved and disappeared to the dining room.

There was no point in telling Dixie that no one was falling for anyone. He and Kenna had only declared a cease-fire and established a tenuous friendship. No one needed to know that the status change had immediately prompted him to thoughts of kissing, but, hey, he'd stopped himself in time.

No harm, no foul.

He could pretend that all he wanted, but he'd seen the expression on Kenna's face. The soft wonder. Whatever he'd felt, she felt it, too... or something like it.

Still, Dixie's parting shot was completely valid. He couldn't just go and fall for a woman who didn't have a deep, personal faith of her own. Dixie had led Dan on a long and painful dance all winter in that regard, and Tony had seen the results up close and personal.

Yeah, there was a big difference. Dan hadn't been a believer, either. They'd lived together for several years and had a baby together before Dan came to the Lord... and Dixie marched in the other direction. For many months, Dan had prayed with little confidence that Dixie would establish a relationship with Jesus and find her way back to him and the kids.

Still, Tony couldn't completely ignore Dixie's warning. That would be a foolhardy choice. His heart already wanted to see where things with Kenna might go. His mind needed to be strong enough to hold himself in check.

14

*K*enna, may I have a word with you?"

Kenna turned to see Winnie standing in the doorway to the garden. "Sure. What's up?" Something must be terribly wrong. Were Marietta's daughters-in-law going to fire her, after all? What terrible thing had she done?

"I was hoping you might enjoy sitting out on the patio. It looks like we've got one last reprieve before it gets too cold."

"Yes. Your mother-in-law is asleep. She will likely nap for another half hour or so. I'm sure she'll hope to see you when she wakens."

Winnie smiled. "I'm glad you're taking such good care of her, Kenna. I know you're just doing your job, and that we're paying you, but it takes such a load off the family to see how well she's being taken care of. I hope you realize how much we value you."

Maybe she wasn't getting fired after all. "Would you like me to put on a pot of tea?" she asked.

"That would be nice. I brought a few cranberry oatmeal cookies for us to share." Winnie settled at the kitchen table while Kenna fixed two cups of tea. If she didn't steep it correctly, Winnie didn't correct her. At least she wasn't expected to make coffee anyone else would want to drink. But her curiosity was killing her.

Winnie chatted about her teenage sons until they were outside. Kenna settled into one of the chairs on the patio. A month ago she would have always chosen to sit in the shade, but now that it was late September, the air was much cooler, and the sunshine was welcome. She nibbled at a cookie and took a sip of tea. "Please tell me what's on your mind."

Winnie chuckled. "I wasn't trying to make you worry. I saw that you were in church on Sunday, and I wondered if that might be the first time you've ever been. What did you think of it?"

Kenna toyed with the hem of her knit dress. How did Winnie know how much she'd been thinking about the pastor's words from last week? Had Marietta told her about their conversation? Kenna wouldn't put it past the old lady. But what did it hurt? Church had definitely been a strange experience.

She studied Winnie for a long moment. The other woman took a sip of her tea and didn't seem about to pressure Kenna in any way. "I haven't stepped foot in a church very often. A few weddings and funerals over the years, and that's about it. The singing was nice. And everyone sure seemed to care about your mother-in-law, even though I think a lot of them were at her birthday party the day before."

Winnie nodded. "Marietta is well loved by the community. Everyone is so glad to see her recovering well, and we have you to thank for it."

"I'm just doing my job," Kenna protested.

"And you're doing it well. What did you think of Pastor Tomas's sermon?"

So the casual conversation had ended, and Winnie was going to keep driving for the heart. Kenna turned her teacup slowly in her hands before looking back at the other woman. "That was a lot of talk about anxiety and fear. I didn't know what to think of it, to be honest."

"I'm sure." Winnie watched a hummingbird whiz by. "The Bible talks about how much God cares for us. He will never leave us or forsake us. And it also says we should cast all our cares on Him, because He cares for us."

Kenna nodded. "That's something like what Marietta mentioned yesterday. She said something about Him working all things for good for people who love God. There was more, but it didn't make sense. How do I know if I love God? I don't even know Him."

"That doesn't change His love for you. It's just like we can feel the effects of the wind without ever seeing what's causing it. Nor can we see the microscopic germs that cause illnesses." Winnie smiled. "To give you an example that might match your experience better."

Kenna studied the hummingbirds buzzing around the feeders. Someone else had been keeping those filled. Was it Tony? Or maybe someone else. "Yes, I definitely believe in germs." She laughed. "But the love of God is stranger than that. First of all, how do I even know God is real and exists?"

"He is willing to show Himself to you," Winnie said softly. "The evidence of Him is all around us just like the evidence of the wind. Or the evidence of germs. We just need to look at the cause and effect in this world, and we will soon come to the realization that a more powerful being must be in charge."

Kenna nodded cautiously. That made sense, even when she was worried about all the evil in the world. It could be so much worse if there was no goodness as well. "I see what you mean. It's hard to completely deny that there's a God. Maurice went to AA for a while, and they told him about a higher power. I don't think he chose to believe it, though."

"And you?"

Kenna sighed. "Okay, yes. I do believe in a higher power. In God, if you will. But the next question is how He loves me. And that is a much bigger stretch for my mind to grasp. I took a lot of science in my training to be a nurse, and it seems like the Bible can't possibly line up with it."

"You'd be surprised. I think if you truly examine the areas where you think science and the Bible are against each other, you'll find that science is either presenting a hypothesis, or that they actually agree. I'd love to leave a book for you to read if you're into it. It's called 'Evidence That Demands a Verdict'." Winnie pulled a paperback out of her purse and laid it on the table between them. "Interested?"

Kenna stared at the book for a long moment before reaching over and running her finger across the cover. Were the Santoros and their neighbors a bunch of wackos? Or was there really something to their faith? She couldn't deny that, regardless of Maurice's opinion, they seemed like one of the kindest, nicest families she'd ever known. Not that she'd ever had much to do with large families like this before. Families where everyone seemed to get along.

Where the mother-in-law and her daughters-in-law respected each other and didn't make nasty, cutting jokes. Where the siblings and the cousins genuinely seemed to like being with each other. She didn't even know what had happened to her own cousins, not that she'd had many. But it sure hadn't been anything like what the Santoro family was like.

She lifted the book and flicked through the pages with her thumb. "I'm curious enough to read this, or at least a little of it. I'll be honest, though. If it's seems like so much hot air, I'll be setting it right back down again."

Winnie nodded. "Fair enough. Let me know what you think when you've had a chance to go through some of it. I know you took Mamma to see the doctor this morning. What did he have to say? Is she healing well?"

Kenna drew in a long breath and let it out slowly. Finally the uncomfortable part of the conversation was over. This part of the conversation was much more up her alley.

⌒ ⸲ ⸱

IT WAS past midnight when Tony opened the gate and entered the backyard. As always, the motion sensor light flicked on at his approach, but what caught his attention was someone sitting in one of the chairs near Nonna's patio door. "Kenna?" Her name escaped his lips without a conscious thought.

She turned to watch him as he came closer. "Hi, Tony."

"You're sure up late. Is something wrong?"

"Not with your grandmother, if that's what you're thinking. Your aunt Winnie came to see me this afternoon."

Tony sat in a chair near Kenna. It was definitely time to

start winding his brain down so he could get some sleep, but he could spare a few minutes for his grandmother's nurse. He tried to ignore the reminder that he had begun to think of her as much more than that. "What about?"

"She wanted to talk to me about God's love." Kenna tugged at the sleeve of her fleece jacket. It definitely was cool outside this late at night.

Tony could do with a jacket himself, but it didn't look like he'd get one. He wouldn't take one to work until the weather turned much colder. The five-minute walk home was barely enough to cool him down after hours in the hot kitchen. He cast a side glance at Kenna. "Aunt Winnie is quite direct. What did she say? What did you think about it?"

Kenna shifted in her seat. "She gave me a book to read." She tapped a paperback lying on the table beside her.

Tony could make out the title just before the motion light winked off, leaving them in the faint glow of a street-light up the block. Wow, Aunt Winnie wasn't pulling any punches. Had she seen signs of readiness that Tony himself had missed? She was so bold in her faith, just like Uncle Al had been. "Did you get a chance to read any of it?"

"A bit," Kenna admitted. "He certainly lays things out systematically."

Tony had to smile at that. "Yes, he does. I've read the book, though it's been a while. I think this might be an updated version, but I'm sure the core of the content is the same. What kinds of questions is it bringing to mind?" Because she had to have questions, or she wouldn't have waited up for him like this. As far as he could tell from the footsteps on the main floor above him, she went to bed much earlier than he did. But then, her workday didn't mesh with his, either. Nonna had always been an early riser, so if Kenna was trying to match her schedule with her client, she would need to do the same.

"Is it true?" she asked softly. "It seems like you would know. Even the introduction makes so much sense. That guy's personal story. It makes me almost afraid to read more."

Tony couldn't see her face in the shadows. He wished he could've at the moment. "Nathan said he talked to Maurice about his need of a Savior before he passed away." Was that something it was okay to remind Kenna of? He didn't even want to think about her married to an alcoholic decades her senior, but it was still a fact of her history.

He could see her turning toward him in the streetlight's glow. "That's the thing, Tony. I heard what Nathan said to him. At least when I was around. And all I could think at the time was, Maurice sure has a lot of things he should be sorry for. And I'm not proud to say I kind of thought that, if God forgave him, it wasn't God's greatest move ever."

This was definitely more than Tony wanted to know about her marriage. "Was he abusive?" He snapped his mouth shut. None of his business. Not a question that he needed to ask, and yet it had shot out of his mouth before he could hold it back.

"Not physically so much," she said at last. "Emotionally, more so. I don't know why I stayed with him. Other than I'm not a quitter."

This time Tony managed to bite his tongue in time. If she wanted to tell him more, that was up to her.

"If God could forgive Maurice, I'm sure He could forgive me. I'm not nearly as bad as him."

"It's not really a question of how bad we've been." Tony

shot a quick prayer heavenward. "God is absolutely perfect. He's never done anything wrong. So just the fact that we've told a little white lie, maybe once in our life, is still enough to separate us from Him. That's why Jesus had to die for our sins. He paid the penalty so that we don't have to. Because of His death, if we accept it, then when God looks at us, all he sees is a reflection of His perfect son, Jesus."

He could make out a small nod. "That makes sense. Kind of. Have you known about this all your life? It seems like you must have with Marietta for a grandmother."

"I did know about it. But my dad wasn't one to toe the party line, which is why he moved away from Bridgeview as a young man. So when I was a kid, I knew about God and about the church, but we weren't regular attenders by any means. My parents made their way back to their faith, but I only found it for myself when I was in Seattle going to culinary school. That's been about ten years now, I guess."

"So you kind of get what's going on in my head. It's all so new. I don't know if it's real, or if it's just some kind of time warp I'm stuck in right now living with your grandmother."

Any dreams of hitting his pillow any second soon vanished in the night breeze. At the moment, Tony didn't care if he slept at all this night. What a privilege to find himself talking to someone who was truly seeking the Lord. And it didn't hurt that this was a woman he'd been coming to respect over the past month and a half since she moved in upstairs. And not only respect, he was finding himself strangely attracted to her.

"Want me to start over at the beginning?"

She nodded.

15

_S_leep evaded Kenna that night. After a couple of hours of listening to Tony talk about Jesus, she'd caught him yawning and realized the man needed his sleep. He wouldn't be able to slack off at Antonio's the next evening just because he was tired from staying up with her.

Then she'd sat on the patio much longer, thinking through what he'd said, what she'd read, and the little else she knew about Christianity from other sources. Small night sounds floated in the still air. A coyote or two yipped near the river a couple of blocks away. The streetlight emitted too much light for a clear view of what was likely a starry night, but she didn't need to see the velvet backdrop studded with rhinestones to know it was there.

She didn't need to see God to know He was there.

The book might offer more proof. It likely did, based on the title and what little she'd read so far. Trying to read more at three in the morning was pointless, though. Her intellect refused to be stimulated, but her emotions settled on what she could feel and sense in the depth of her being.

She wanted to blame God for her upbringing. She wanted to blame Him for the Maurice years. But then she remembered the abuse the author, Josh McDowell, had undergone from both his father and their farm helper. Josh had forgiven both men.

That's when she'd put the book down to marvel at it. The author hadn't submerged his memories and moved on from them. He'd faced them. Faced the men. Acknowledged the horrific pain he'd experienced at their hands.

And forgiven them.

The glint of dawn filtered through Kenna's curtains before she'd finished grappling with that. The author considered that step vital to his growth, but when she thought of her own father and her late husband, she wasn't so sure she could go through with it herself. She'd been hurt. Badly. Forgiving the perpetrators felt like saying it didn't matter.

It did matter.

But the boy Josh had been through worse and managed to forgive.

God? Is it necessary? For the first time, the episodes flashing through her mind felt like a ball and chain around her ankle. They held her back. Held her down from flying. She envisioned unbuckling the chain — who knew she'd had the power to do that? — grabbed ahold of a big bunch of helium balloons, and floated into the sky. This was a whole new perspective.

The author said it wasn't, in fact, his own power that had removed the chain. It was God's.

And then Kenna's thoughts shifted. Forgiveness didn't change the past, and it wasn't something within her ability. She could say the words, but the power of the past would still be there. Unless God was much, much stronger than she was.

Light brightened her room, and a shaft of sunlight hit the framed photo of her wedding to Maurice. The one she'd set up to remind her she wasn't worthy of joy. Wasn't worthy of new love. But God said she was. Not because she was so great on her own, but because of Jesus.

Kenna swung her legs over the edge of her bed and wrapped her robe around herself. She studied the photo of the naive girl and the alcoholic who'd already been divorced three times. She'd assumed she could save him.

She hadn't been able to. And it hadn't taken many weeks before she didn't even want to try anymore. Her words to Tony last night rang in her memory. *I'm not a quitter.*

There were times a person should quit. She should have left Maurice long before the cirrhosis made itself known, but all that ugliness was in her past. Maurice had gone to his reward, such as it was. He wouldn't ever know if she forgave him or not. Neither would her father, since he'd committed suicide in Kenna's teens.

So the forgiveness was only for her, to unfetter her from the ball and chain.

She touched Maurice's face on the photo. "You hurt me, over and over. You didn't know how to love anyone but yourself. Even there, you did a lousy job. Somehow you were only happy when you'd made sure no one else could be, but it didn't bring the results you wanted. Not really. You were trapped in your own loop, misery adding to misery."

He'd told her a bit about his early years. About his mother. About his other wives. Those situations didn't excuse the man he'd become, but they did offer some insight.

"I don't know if I can forgive you," she told his image. "On my own, I'm pretty sure I can't, actually. But I'm going to try this Jesus thing, and maybe He can help. Because my hate isn't bothering you any — not anymore — but it's sure holding me back. I want to fly free."

Kenna opened the bottom drawer and put the frame inside, face down. She slipped out of her room and into the bathroom across the hall. Then she heard Marietta rustling in her bed through the app.

Morning already? Maybe today, instead of additional questions, she'd find answers. No doubt her client would be happy to help.

IT WAS NEARLY ELEVEN before Tony let himself into his grandmother's place upstairs. He didn't usually go there anymore, or at least he hadn't until this week when he and Kenna had agreed on friendship. After last night, he felt like they had approached a new level in their relationship, and he wanted to see how she was feeling about everything she'd confided in him in the dark of night. Besides, Nonna always appreciated his visits, even if Kenna had not.

Kenna dropped a small zucchini on the floor. "Oh, you startled me!"

"Oops." Tony grinned as she scooped it up and ran it under the faucet. "I didn't mean to make you throw vegetables around the kitchen."

"Antonio! Is that you?" came Nonna's voice from the other room.

Tony offered another apologetic smile to Kenna and headed through the archway into the living room. Aunt

Grace sat beside Nonna, and it looked like they'd been coming up with a plan by the smile on both their faces.

"Tony, how're things going?" asked Aunt Grace. "Mamma and I were just talking about getting everyone together this weekend again to keep going through things in the basement. Are you up for cooking?"

Something inside him snapped. "This weekend? Not really. I've got a lot going on." More than that, he wanted *different* things to be going on. It seemed as though his aunts were taking advantage of his abilities and good nature. That didn't mean he wanted to cook for the family incessantly. Sometimes it felt like he was their servant instead of their nephew. Would they ask Jasmine or Daria or Fran to cook all the time? Not a chance. And it wasn't only because those cousins didn't have the same credentials Tony did. They just wouldn't dream of asking.

"Oh. I just thought…" It was clear Aunt Grace had no idea what to say next.

Nonna's eyebrows rose. If she was going to start with the whole thing about how she'd given him a place to stay, he would definitely take the time to find a place of his own soon. Wasn't it enough that the aunts and uncles went straight through his part of the basement every time they wanted something from the storage room? And now they were in and out of there constantly. He had no privacy.

Well, these were not his usual thoughts. And yet he couldn't find anything wrong with them per se. It might be just the fact that he'd had so little sleep the night before. That removed the amount of patience he had for anything he hadn't chosen to do. Oh, yes, he needed to remember that he owed his uncles a large debt for all the work they'd done to get the restaurant renovated and ready for operation. He was under no illusions about that. It would've taken him another five years at least to figure out how to do this without his family's help. But that still didn't mean they'd earned the right to take advantage of him every time he turned around.

"Would you like a cup of coffee?" Nonna asked, as though changing the subject would make any difference.

"No thanks. I was just checking in to see how you were doing this morning. I have a lot to do today, so I'll get going on it now." Tony turned and headed back into the kitchen.

Kenna stared at him with wide eyes, her mouth open in astonishment. "Are you okay?"

Tony swallowed hard and willed his frustration to dissipate. It wasn't Kenna's fault, not even a little bit. And usually he was fine with less sleep than normal. He just hadn't been able to rest well after he got inside last night, thinking of her still sitting there, considering whether the Bible was true and God was real. If anything, he should be far more patient with her today... and with everyone else.

"I'm good. How are you? Did you get any sleep?"

"Not so you'd notice." She gave a small self-deprecating laugh. "The next thing I knew, daylight was sneaking in the windows. I hope you slept better than I did."

"Probably not. I couldn't stop thinking about our conversation and praying for you. I asked God to reveal himself to you, and give you just enough faith to reach for His hand. I know He'll do the rest if you only let Him."

"I read in that book that you really need to be willing to forgive people. That seems like a gigantic step. I'm not sure I'm ready to take it."

And here Tony had just been a little rude to his aunt and grandmother, probably something he was going to need to apologize for. He hated when that happened. "If you need someone to talk to before three o'clock, come find me."

Kenna's eyebrows rose. "I thought it sounded like you were very busy today and all week."

Tony closed his eyes then opened them again. He glanced toward the living room and lowered his voice, stepping closer to Kenna so the other women wouldn't overhear. "Not too tired or busy for you." He searched her face.

Kenna's lips parted as her eyes widened. "Did you just make that up?"

"Not really. It's true that I don't have time to cook dinner for ten people this weekend. Life has been really stressful, and I need a break." She probably needed one, too. "What do you say? Maybe we could go for a hike or a bike ride or something on Saturday. We can ask one of my aunts to sit in if you prefer."

Wait, had he just asked Kenna on a date? The invitation to Antonio's had been different. That had been more to show her what he did at work so she'd understand who he was and what made him the way he was. But an invitation like this was definitely more. That didn't mean he didn't mean it. Wow, he should back off. Just because she was making some headway in seeking out God didn't mean it was time to start dating her.

"I'm not sure I can do that. It sounds as though your aunts will be too busy sorting things in the basement to ask one of them to sit with your grandmother. And anywhere off the property is farther than I want to go while she's napping, unless someone is with her."

"Of course. I wasn't thinking. You're far more tied to your work than I am to mine. I shouldn't have asked."

She stretched her hand toward him then let it fall away. "No apology needed. I'm just not sure this is a good time."

Tony felt a flush creep up his neck. He could read between the lines as well as anyone else. What she really meant was she didn't know if it was a good time for them to start going out. Probably that meant he'd imagined a little bit of awareness she'd seemed to have for him. For some crazy reason, she'd become embedded in his thoughts. He couldn't help wondering what she was thinking, what she wanted out of life, what made her tick. He had a pretty good idea what made her ticked *off*, but that wasn't the same thing. And now he'd gone and messed up any chance they had for that friendship he'd professed to want only a week ago.

Tony backed up a couple of steps and put his hand on the patio doorknob.

"No problem. I'll ask Peter or Alex if they want to go. Or I haven't played any three-on-three in quite a while. My cousins are always up for that." He opened the patio door. "Don't worry about it. Still, I hope you'll plan to come down to Antonio's one evening and have dinner in the kitchen. It's the staff table, and there's often one of the servers taking a break there, so it's not completely private."

Why had he said that about being private? Would she think he meant the two of them? That's not what he'd meant at all. Obviously, his mouth did not consult with his brain before speaking if he hadn't had enough sleep. That wasn't good for anyone. Not for him and Nonna and Aunt Grace, and definitely not for him and Kenna.

Except there was no him and Kenna. He needed to remember that.

16

She hadn't seen Tony this out of sorts in the six weeks since the first time she met him. Whatever it was that she managed to say wrong a couple of days ago in Marietta's kitchen, she had no idea. She thought they'd really connected the night before talking out on the patio for so long. But then he'd been so short with his grandmother and aunt, made an overture toward Kenna, and then backed off completely when she gave him a very real reason why she couldn't drop everything and go for a hike with him. Sure, there was more to it than that. She was almost tempted to put Maurice's picture back up in her room, to remind herself that getting interested in a man again was a very bad idea. She had goals for her life. They definitely didn't include marrying again. Once was more than enough, something Maurice had never figured out. How he had managed to convince not one, but four, women to marry him was still hard to figure out.

How had she been so duped by him? Sure, he'd put on the charm, but there really hadn't been that much charm.

Yet she had fallen for him. It definitely had not been love. There was no mutual respect or joint interests or anything really other than that initial flare of sexual attraction. She's gotten over that in a big fat hurry, but it had been too late. She was Makenna Hamelin, and she didn't take that lightly. For some reason she thought she, of all Maurice's wives, would be the one to make him into a new man. Other wives would come to see that it wasn't only him who was to blame. They were also to blame for their failed marriages. Nathan's mom had disappeared, never to be heard from again. The next wife had been smart enough to pack up her two sons and leave after only five years. Not that the other woman had done a much better job of raising her boys without Maurice. And young Jason's mom had divorced Maurice but then gone on to die of cancer, which sent Jason back to his father until the man's untimely death. If it wasn't for his big brother Nathan, Jason would have become just another statistic of a broken home and messed-up parents.

One thing, Kenna had known all along she wouldn't give Maurice children. No amount of controlling on his part could change the fact that she was barren, the result of a hysterectomy when she was a teenager. Cancer. Not that she'd told Maurice. It hadn't been any of his business. He already had four sons by three different women, and had proven to be a horrible father to all four of them.

Kenna hadn't much cared whether she ever became a mother or not. Not after her mother had turned a blind eye to the way her dad had treated her. Not after her dad's suicide. Not after seeing so many children in the pediatrics wards at the hospital, victims of abuse. She was just as glad she wasn't going to be adding to the world's population and its problems.

Tony, on the other hand, always seemed to have one of his cousin's children in his arms, like Jasmine's daughter, Lillian. Or he'd be roughhousing with Marco's three boys. And then there was the time his sister Gina had been in town, and Tony had handled her kids like a natural. Probably a man like Tony would want children of his own.

That right there was the perfect reason to keep avoiding him the way he was avoiding her. For that brief week, it had been nice to have a friend, but since then, he'd started avoiding her again as he had before. It was probably just as well.

Kenna tapped on her phone and called Carol. When her coworker answered, Kenna asked, "Hey, how are things going?"

"Kenna! Good to hear from you. I was going to give you a call since it's near the end of September. Am I okay to keep living in your apartment for a while longer? Dave and I have been going to counseling, but I'm not ready to move back to the house anytime soon."

"My contract with Mrs. Santoro has been extended. She's not healing as quickly as the doctors had at first hoped, so I'm needed here. Which means that you're welcome to my apartment for a while longer. Are you sure about going back to Dave, though? I thought he'd been abusive and that you were well rid of him."

Carol hesitated. "He said he's sorry. It seems as though I should give him the benefit of the doubt."

The hairs on the back of Kenna's neck bristled. "It's pretty rare for a guy like that to change all of a sudden," she cautioned.

"They are willing to say just about anything to get the victim back in their clutches." How many times had Dad promised Mom things would be different now? Too many to count.

"He seems sincere. The counseling has been good for both of us, so we'll see."

Kenna could all but see Carol's shoulder shrug. "Just be careful, okay? Statistics are against you. Or against this working out."

"Says the woman who stayed with a real jerk for six years."

Hard to deny. "Either way, you're welcome to the apartment for the month of October. Why not go ahead and plan on November as well? I can't see any hope of me being able to leave Mrs. Santoro before Thanksgiving at the earliest."

"Okay, that does take some of the pressure off. We'll keep going to counseling and see how things work out. I'll let you know when I've got a final plan."

Kenna said goodbye and tapped to end the call. She stared at her cell phone for a long moment. Why couldn't Carol learn from someone else's mistakes? Not even just Kenna's. There was a long list of people they both knew whose situations had gone from bad to worse. What was with society these days, anyway?

They've walked away from God, figuring they can do everything on their own.

The thought came unbidden into Kenna's head. But it was still true. In the Little House on the Prairie days people tended to go to church. They believed in God and said grace before meals. Had that made them a better society?

Tony was like that. He was probably rethinking getting

involved with someone like her. Someone who had so many questions. Someone who didn't have life put together.

There was no chance he knew she was unable to have children. But if he found that out, things between them would definitely be over. Of course, they already were. They had no relationship to *be* over. It was definitely time she dragged Maurice's picture back out of the drawer one more time, set it on her dresser, and used it as a shield against Tony and anyone else. She'd remember. She wouldn't make the same mistake twice. Maybe Jesus could rescue her, but she doubted He would bother to replace her womb.

TONY SHOT the basketball at Peter, who dribbled in and dodged past Alex before shooting the ball back to Tony for a layup.

Swish.

He slapped Peter's hand, and Alex sent the ball back into the court, straight at Marco. Peter got into Marco's way and stole the ball, but Alex snatched it back.

Swish.

Tony had missed this. Missed hanging out with his cousins building up a sweat. It might be late September, but the rain from earlier in the week had cleared away, leaving a mellow sunshine in its wake.

"Time," yelled Evan as he jogged toward the bench to glug down half a bottle of water.

Tony took the moment to rest his hands on his knees and catch his breath.

Peter slugged him on the back. "Out of shape, chef?"

"For sure. On my feet a lot but not so much with the cardio."

"Ha. Yeah, if I didn't play three-on-three a couple of nights a week, I'd turn into a blob."

"I doubt it. Not with all the gardening you do. Lots of workout in that, I'm sure."

Peter shrugged. "As you said, not a lot of cardio. Maybe a bit more strenuous than chopping shallots, though."

Tony took a swing at Peter's head, but his cousin ducked away, grinning. No need to tell the guy that he rarely chopped anything. That was what Oriana was for, not him.

Alex glanced at his watch. "Are we playing another round or not? I promised Marley I'd help out with building her chicken coop this afternoon."

And Tony needed to shower and head down to Antonio's within the next hour. "Probably not. But guys, I can't thank you enough. I know you're all busy, but I appreciate you all responding to my rallying cry."

"Dude, I didn't know you missed playing. Sorry about that." Peter rubbed a towel across his neck. "It's just everyone else works in the daytime so we hit the court after supper, most nights."

"I know. My schedule's weird."

"But an occasional break on a Saturday afternoon is good." Evan stuffed his empty water bottle into the side pocket of his gear bag. "Especially now with the weather cooling off into fall."

The youngest of Uncle Ray and Aunt Grace's five kids, Evan was in his final year of law school. His body didn't look like he spent all his time eating chips and ice cream while he studied, though.

"I've got to run Caden and Oren to jiu jitsu soon."

Marco pulled on a pair of track pants over his shorts. "And then I'm sure Daria's got a honey-do list for me." He grinned at Tony. "Nice of you to give me an excuse to get out for a bit, chef."

"Ditto." Nathan stretched. "Jasmine's spending the day canning tomatoes with Fran at Rebecca's. Tieri's watching the little ones."

Their cousin Fran's daughter was only eight, but she was a well-experienced babysitter since her mom ran a home daycare. With Jasmine right there to intervene as needed, Lillian would bask in Tieri's attention, as would Rebecca and Wade's one-year-old, Theodore.

"Next week again?" Tony asked hopefully.

The guys looked at each other, nodding. "I'll double check we don't have anything else going on," said Marco. "Besides the jiu jitsu."

Even though he needed to start prepping for work soon, Tony hated to leave the guys. He hadn't known he needed this reprieve. Sure, he saw them Thursday mornings at the prayer breakfast, but he was generally too tired to participate much after only four or five hours of sleep. And the guys were right. How could they know how much he missed hanging out if he never said anything? They'd grown up here without him, after all. Their circle likely felt complete without his presence, even though they were happy to include him when reminded.

It was up to Tony to remind them. To show himself a friend and comrade, not just a cousin who happened to live with their grandmother. He slung his sports bag over one shoulder but wasn't surprised when Nathan fell into step beside him. If Nathan was meeting up with Jasmine, he'd be walking the same direction as Tony.

"How're things?" Nathan cast a sidelong glance at Tony.

"All right." Confusing, but no need to burden Nathan with that.

"How's Makenna doing with Nonna?"

Tony had come to think of her as Kenna over the past month or so. At least the question was how she was doing with Nonna, not him. "Good. She's very attentive and seems to know when to push Nonna with PT and when to ease off."

"Excellent. Is she letting you in the kitchen yet?" Nathan elbowed him, grinning.

Why had he ever told anyone how frustrated he was about that way back at the beginning? "Some." No need to explain how they'd even cooked together last Sunday... or how he'd abdicated when next invited. No doubt Nathan already knew. Word traveled instantaneously in this clan.

"I keep praying for her. She put up with my Pops for so long, I feel like I owe her a debt of gratitude. It seems like she's built a tough-woman barricade, but behind it, I think she's really confused and hurting."

Tony found himself nodding. "She's asking questions about faith."

"She is? Wow, I'm glad." Then Nathan stopped on the sidewalk and stared at him. "Who's she talking to? You?"

Tony'd gone and done it, now. "Some. But Aunt Winnie started it, loaning her that Josh McDowell book."

"Good for Winnie." Nathan searched Tony's face then shook his head. "But Makenna's talking to you about it? Thought you two were sworn enemies."

"She's not so bad." Oh, that was lame. A guy just off the brink of hate should not have had a single thought about kissing a woman. "She's devoted to Nonna."

"So you said." Nathan chuckled. "You're not falling for her, are you?"

Tony forced a laugh. "I'm too busy with the restaurant to have a love life, I assure you."

"Famous last words. If anyone would understand a schedule like yours, it would be a nurse. Hers was even crazier when she worked at the hospital. Twelve-hour days, twelve-hour nights. I'd say it would be even harder to date a nurse than a chef."

"See? It would never work." Tony kept his voice light, but Nathan's words found their mark. How many times had Kenna talked about her love of nursing in his hearing? Enough that he knew she valued her career. That wasn't likely to change if she made a decision to follow Jesus. The two areas of life were complementary, not opposed.

But where did that leave Tony? Married to his restaurant. He'd known when he signed on that it would be at least five years before he could relax the slightest bit. Nothing had changed in that regard.

17

I'm Kenna Johnson. The chef is expecting me."
The words sounded strange to her own ears, but
no stranger than the opulent Tuscan villa she'd stepped into.
She felt like Alice stepping into Wonderland or Dorothy
being dropped into Oz. *We're not in Spokane anymore, Toto.*

"Right this way." The maître d' bowed slightly and beckoned her to follow him. They wove past several semi-private
nooks adorned with glistening chandeliers above tables for
two. One had a tall, narrow waterfall cascading into a stone
basin at the bottom. Another had a fireplace.

But then the maître d' opened a swinging door and
ushered her into a gleaming kitchen in a back corner of the
building and pointed her to an alcove by a window overlooking the Spokane River. Two high-backed, padded
benches flanked a wide-planked table big enough for six.
"Have a seat. The chef will be right with you."

Kenna slid onto the bench and angled herself so she
could see Tony at work. He gave her a grin but remained

focused on the row of plates between him and the young woman working at the next station over.

Who was that? Kenna's eyes narrowed for a second before she remembered it was not only none of her business, but that she had no claim on Tony at all. She was here at his invitation, but only as friends. That's all they would ever be, and she'd be wise to keep that at the forefront.

But he was a fine man to watch in his white coat and pleated hat. He moved quickly, efficiently, as he plated the order. His assistant seemed in charge of the side dishes, and they worked together with few words.

But Kenna's gaze slid back to Tony. To the ripple of his shoulders as he moved, to the precision as he squeezed sauce across the plate in an obviously rehearsed pattern. He nodded to his assistant, and she transferred the plates to the ledge facing the dining room. "Table four up!" she called as she pressed a bell.

Tony tapped the tablet in front of him and scrolled. Seemingly satisfied, he turned toward Kenna. "Ready to be served?" he asked with a grin, his blue eyes gleaming even across the space.

"Sure." Butterflies danced in her belly. Not so much in anticipation of the food, but at the personal attention. She'd had so little of that in her life. "Do I pick from the menu?"

Tony's smile widened, revealing his dimple. "Not at all. You get the Chef Special."

Somehow, she was robbed of air. "Okay."

"I hope you're hungry." He turned back to his workstation and said something to his assistant she couldn't hear. The woman glanced at Kenna with a curious expression.

A few minutes later, Tony set a plate in front of her with

a slight bow. "For your appetizer tonight, Clams Oreganata. I hope you enjoy."

The aroma filtered upward, mixing with the fragrance that was all Tony. Kenna found her gaze welded to his for a few seconds. "Thank you. This smells amazing." Truth was, she hadn't yet done so much as glance at it. Her attention was all on the chef.

And to think she'd kicked him out of his grandmother's kitchen while she burned the old lady's food. She'd been getting a bit better at it, though. Marietta had coached her enough to keep the bottoms of eggs golden brown instead of crisp black. Runny yolks were nothing but a horror, though. How could they possibly be safe, even though Marietta assured her Marley's chickens were as healthy as they could be?

It wasn't until Tony turned back to his kitchen that Kenna took a longer look at the clams perched in their little shells in front of her. She'd never been one for dining out a lot. This wasn't the sort of place a woman came with girl-friends, even if she had anyone close. Maurice had certainly been too tight-fisted to splurge on a fancy meal.

Well, she was here now, in a ringside seat, and she'd make the most of it. And that included digging into the deliciousness in front of her... although the clams were a strange texture. She nudged that thought out of her mind along with the other sounds, smells, and sights from the kitchen proper, and focused on the unique blend of flavors.

Not that she could completely keep her eyes off Tony. He glanced over several times, meeting her gaze with an acknowledging smile that also seemed to gauge her reactions and progress with the appetizer, because as soon as she'd set the fork down after her final bite, he came over to remove the plate.

"A glass of wine?"

She shook her head. Watching Maurice's liver shut down from decades of alcohol abuse had been enough to swear her off it for life. "Ginger ale, maybe. Or water is fine."

He nodded and spoke to someone through the gap to the dining room. A moment later Dixie Ranta appeared with a glass clinking with ice cubes. "Hi, Kenna. Here's your ginger ale."

"Thank you." Kenna didn't want to examine the younger woman's gaze. Dixie hesitated a moment, likely curious, then headed out of the kitchen through the swinging doors.

Tony approached with two plates. He set one in front of her and slid in across from her with the other. "Things have slowed down, so I'll take a break, too. May I say grace?"

She nodded and bowed her head then listened to his short prayer of thanks. A bed of noodles — or was that something else? — was covered with a creamy sauce dotted with sausage and green stuff. Kale, maybe? "This smells amazing."

"I hope it tastes the same." He twirled his fork. "How were the clams?"

"Amazing." She'd already used that word. She had a strange feeling she'd use it a few more times by the end of the evening.

That dimple appeared again as his eyes crinkled. "I'm glad. It's one of our most popular starters, so I took a chance you'd enjoy it." He pointed his fork at her plate. "Ditto on the zucchini noodles with the andouille sauce. Lots of people are flirting with a ketogenic diet these days."

So she'd been right. Not pasta after all. But she

couldn't fault the taste. She sighed against her fork as the full flavor activated all the taste buds in her mouth. "You're good."

His blue eyes intensified. "You're not just saying that?"

She couldn't tear her gaze away. "It's the best meal I've had in... I can't even remember. Possibly ever."

"Well, you know how to get to a man's heart." Then he seemed to realize what he'd said.

The air seemed charged between them for a long moment before Kenna managed to disengage and focus on loading her fork for another bite.

Wowzah. This man was deadly. To her heart.

THE REST of the evening was fairly slow, even for a Wednesday, so Tony lingered at the staff table while Oriana prepped for the next day. There was a little rush by a group of concertgoers just before ten, and he got up to fix their orders.

Kenna didn't seem in any hurry to leave, even as she savored her tiramisu then finally nudged her empty plate away. Her curious gaze followed him around the kitchen.

He was accustomed to being watched but, with Kenna, it was different. She wasn't trying to learn a technique or analyze his choreography or critique his flavors. She just... watched.

Tony didn't dare become distracted. Thankfully the orders were meals he could practically cook in his sleep, and Oriana was attentive to add the correct sides and salads. She was finally shaking down into a good sous chef.

When the group had been served, it was nearly time to

close. Tony slid back into the booth and set his hat on the table. It was hard to stay away.

"What did you think?" He left the question open-ended.

"Impressive." Her gray eyes sought his.

"It's only fifteen minutes until closing. If you want, I'll walk you home then."

She glanced over at Oriana, who was scraping down the griddle. "You don't have to stay and finish cleanup?"

He shook his head. "Not tonight. I'll come in a bit early tomorrow to make sure everything's ready. The servers have already cleaned everywhere but those final tables, and Derrick will make sure those are ready before he locks up. I don't need to be the last one out the door." It wasn't that many weeks ago when things had changed. Hiring Dixie had been a good move. She was an instinctively good server and the other waitstaff emulated her.

Maybe Antonio's would be up for that award in January after all. If so, Dixie deserved a good part of the credit.

"Okay," Kenna said softly.

It took Tony a minute to realize she was agreeing to walking back to the house together. He kept the small talk rolling while keeping an eye on the clock. As soon as Derrick assured him the restaurant was empty and the doors locked, Tony stood and shucked his white coat. "Got the rest of the prep?" he asked Oriana.

His assistant nodded, casting a curious glance between him and Kenna. He could hardly blame Oriana. He'd never invited anyone other than staff into the kitchen in the past six months. But Oriana was going to have to hold her thoughts. Tony wasn't all that sure what was going on, either. But he did know he'd thrived on having Kenna in his space. Thrived on making an entree just for her and sharing a meal with her away from the awkwardness in Nonna's kitchen due to their history.

"Ready?" He held out his hand to Kenna. He'd meant it as a gesture, but a thrill ran through him when she grasped it and slid out of the booth. Then he didn't want to let go. It wasn't far to the backdoor, and he could come back in the morning for his messenger bag. So he simply held the door for her and escorted her onto the riverfront pathway behind the restaurant. And he didn't let go.

Kenna let out a long sigh as they strolled under the starry sky. A few lamps lit the pathway as well.

Tony held his breath as he twined his fingers through hers. Too much, too soon? He'd been telling himself for two weeks that anything between them was a bad idea, but underneath it all, he couldn't help but wonder if that was true. How could he know for sure if he didn't give it a try and see where it might lead? She might shoot him down.

So far, she wasn't doing that. Just the opposite.

He glanced over in the moonlight and found her sneaking a peek as well. He stopped and turned toward her.

She was wearing the lower-heeled soft-soled shoes and a casual tunic over leggings tonight, and her blond hair fell in soft waves over her shoulders.

Tony couldn't resist reaching up with his free hand and tucking the locks behind her ear. "Kenna?"

She looked away, and her fingers convulsed in his. "I don't think this is a good idea."

"Why not?" Oh, he knew. He could list a hundred reasons in as many seconds. At the moment, he didn't much care about any of them. His fingers trailed down her cheek, down her arm, and rested against her slim waist.

"You don't like me, remember?" She peeked at him.

Tony grinned. "I've completely forgotten why." And with that, he shifted just a little closer and set his other hand on her other hip, tugging her gently toward him.

She met him halfway, her fingers bunching the front of his T-shirt as he drew her into his arms.

He barely needed to tip his head to touch his lips to hers. Delicious electricity zinged through him, and Kenna quivered as though she felt it, too. But then he closed his mouth over hers and kissed her the way he'd been dreaming of ever since that day in the basement apartment.

She tasted of chocolate and whipped cream with a hint of garlic and spice and a flavor that was all Kenna.

Not that Tony had gone around kissing dozens of women. Until he'd met this one, he'd kept a friendly distance, his eyes always on the prize of owning his own restaurant. Tonight, he didn't much care. The culinary award could come to him or someone else, and it didn't matter. The fate of Antonio's didn't matter. It didn't need to be the top startup of the calendar year. It was a good restaurant. Solid.

And the woman in his arms was good and solid in her own right. She kissed him back for what might have been minutes or hours before she pulled away. "Tony, are you going to regret this tomorrow?"

He cupped his hands around her shoulders and looked deeply into her eyes. "Not at all. Will you?"

"I hope not," she whispered. "But I'm not certain."

Tony kissed her again. Maybe he could persuade her this was meant to be.

18

*A*ll night she'd relived Tony's kisses. All morning she'd performed her duties to Marietta without thinking about them too deeply. She loaded Marietta into the car and took her to the doctor for her regular visit.

When they returned to the house, Winnie met them at the door. She leaned down and gently kissed her mother-in-law on both cheeks. "How was your appointment, Mamma?"

"It is good, I think." Marietta plucked at the cast on her arm. "Soon I will be rid of this, but not soon enough."

"I'm glad your arm is healing. And the rest of you?"

The old woman sighed. "The ribs are better because I cannot do anything to injure them since I cannot move."

Kenna patted her client's shoulder. "So that's a silver lining."

Winnie smiled at Kenna. "I like your attitude."

Yeah, it had definitely improved over the past six weeks, and it had improved exponentially last night. She couldn't help but be buoyed by Tony's optimism that everything would work out as it was meant to, even knowing full well she didn't deserve a positive outcome.

Winnie held the door open as Kenna wheeled Marietta inside. "How did you like your visit to Antonio's last night?"

Did Kenna really have to answer that? Probably. Grace had likely told everyone she'd sat with Marietta for a couple of hours, to say nothing of Kenna having returned a bit later than expected. Marietta had long been asleep, but Grace hadn't chided Kenna. She'd only closed her paperback, tucked it in her bag, and headed out the door with a smile and a wave.

"It was very interesting. I've never sat in a restaurant kitchen before. It's a busy place, though Tony said it was a relatively quiet evening."

Winnie smiled. "He's done a good job, our Tony."

As if Kenna could ever forget he was related to half of Bridgeview, even though his sister's family and his parents didn't live here. What would it be like to suddenly be related to so many people?

Not that she'd have to worry about that. This thing with Tony would only be a brief interlude. Once his grandmother didn't need a nurse anymore, they'd drift apart... if Tony hadn't already realized his mistake by that time.

She settled Marietta in the living room and went to her room to change.

The thought of a family like this one was strangely enticing. Peter's fiancée, Sadie, was an only child whose mother had passed away. She seemed to revel in the craziness that was the Santoro clan. And now Alex had a serious girlfriend who also had no family.

Moths to a flame, but Kenna would hold back. Other people had the happily-ever-afters. They didn't come to women like her. Unless she counted Maurice's death. That had been a blessing she hadn't expected in the first few years, though she'd prayed for it.

As though God had knocked him dead because of her insipid prayers. She hadn't had a clue about God back then. She traced the cover of the book Winnie had given her. If the book was true, then the Bible was true. And if the Bible was true, then God loved her and didn't spend His days laughing at her discomfort. In fact, He'd even welcome her if she accepted His love. Then she'd be part of His family.

Like the Santoros, only bigger and better.

Huh. If she hadn't walled herself off so completely, she could ask Sadie or Marley what it was like to find a family in Jesus-followers, let alone their boyfriends' family. But Winnie was here. Winnie had opened the conversation and given her the book.

Kenna headed back to the living room where Marietta sat looking out onto the street. In the kitchen, the moka coffee maker hissed and gurgled. Not long ago, Kenna would have insisted she could fix her client's coffee without help. But, seriously, what was the issue? Under normal circumstances, family would pitch in. No big deal.

"Hey, Kenna!" Winnie looked up from pouring the coffee with a smile. Then she glanced toward the living room and lowered her voice. "Is she really doing well? Anything we should know?"

And then something else struck Kenna. When she was eighty and broke some bones, who would be there to care for her? She wouldn't have five daughters-in-law and a raft of grandchildren and great-grandchildren popping in and out to brighten her day and smear peanut butter on the low windows as Gavin did. There'd be her and her nurse, just the two of them. In her mind's eye, the nurse looked strangely like Tony.

Could she really give in to this fantasy and believe they could build a future? But kids still were never going to be an option. He'd care about that. She knew he would.

Kenna met Winnie's gaze. "The doctor is pleased with her progress this time. It will still be a few weeks before that cast comes off. By then, her ribs should be completely healed and her pelvis ready for limited mobility. So, yes, she's definitely on the mend."

"I'm glad to hear that. I can't tell you how thankful the whole family is for you. You're an answer to prayer."

Such a strange thought, right on the heels of what she'd been thinking. "Prayer... does that do any good?"

Winnie set down the moka maker. "It definitely does. God hears and answers."

"How can you say that? Didn't people pray for Al to get well after his accident?"

The other woman's smile remained steady, though her eyes misted slightly. "So many people prayed."

"And God didn't answer."

"He did answer. We asked for Him to heal Al if it was His will. And if it wasn't, that God would be glorified in Al's death."

That just sounded like a cop-out. "I don't get it."

"Bad things happen on this planet every day. I'm sure I don't need to start making a list of those."

Kenna shook her head.

"But that doesn't mean God has abdicated control. He's given us free will. The woman who ran into Al's truck exercised her free will to drink and drive."

"You must hate her."

"No. It was a struggle to forgive her at first, but I couldn't imagine the pain she felt knowing her foolish action had taken someone's life."

Seriously? Winnie should be awarded sainthood.

"Kenna, my husband loved Jesus with his whole heart. He shared his faith with everyone he met. I know he led dozens of people to God during his life... but even more in his death. Hundreds of people came to his celebration of life. Pastor Tomas presented the good news of Jesus clearly. Honestly, though? Many of those people had heard it before. From Al. And now they were ready to believe. You've met Wesley Ferguson, haven't you?"

Kenna tried to remember who he was. "The sculptor?"

"Yes. He's married to Kass, one of the owners of Bridgeview Bakery and Bistro. He came to faith because of Al's testimony. So did Dan Ranta, and that brought Dixie and several of her friends. Those are just a few examples of people you might know. Cards and emails and phone calls came in for months from people telling me how much Al had meant to them. I still get an occasional one two years later."

What a legacy. It seemed a person didn't need to have kids and grandkids to be someone remembered and revered. How would Kenna be remembered? Would anyone even care if she passed on?

"Most important, though, is the woman who killed Al. I've had the honor of meeting her. Praying with her. Forgiving her."

"I don't get it, Winnie. I really don't. But I want to."

"Jesus wants you to welcome Him into your life. Are you ready?"

She nodded. "I'm ready."

TONY'D SEEN Kenna's car come back not long before he needed to leave for Antonio's. He'd also seen Aunt Winnie's car, which had been enough to keep him from checking in with Kenna. If things were going to be awkward after those kisses last night, he didn't want Aunt Winnie or Nonna around to witness it.

And if things were *not* going to be awkward? He also didn't need witnesses.

So he wasn't completely surprised when he slipped through the gate late that night after closing Antonio's and caught sight of Kenna sitting in the shadows huddled in a fuzzy blanket. "Hi," he said softly, stopping at the edge of the grape arbor.

"Hi. Do you have a minute?"

His heart warmed. "For you? Absolutely. But do you mind if I run down and grab a hoodie first?"

"Go for it."

He returned a moment later, but she didn't rise to meet him. What did that tell him? That she hadn't spent the past twenty-four hours wondering when they could kiss again? He bent down and swept his lips over hers.

She kissed him back but didn't reach for him.

Okay. Mixed signals. Since when was that anything new with her? He settled into the patio chair beside hers and laid his hand on the arm, palm up. Kenna nestled her hand inside his, and he stroked the back of her hand with his thumb. This would be enough for now. And talking was probably good. "What's on your mind?"

"A couple of things. One of them is your grandmother had her checkup this afternoon."

"And? Is she doing as well as it seems?"

Kenna's nod was just visible in the streetlight's glow. "Another few weeks and the cast on her arm will come off. The ribs are pretty much healed. The pelvis is doing as well as can be expected. It's probably just as well she broke her arm, to be honest. It's helped keep her immobilized and allowed the other bones to heal that couldn't be set."

"That's good." He toyed with her fingers. "Right?"

"Yes." She hesitated. "Winnie was here."

"Um hmm?" Tony leaned back and closed his eyes. He'd need to watch that he didn't fall asleep with her comforting hand in his.

"She told me about her husband and how so many people became believers because of him."

A second wind flowed over him. "He was a remarkable man. All of Spokane loved Uncle Al."

"That's what she said. And she forgave the woman who killed him. I-I don't know if I could have done that."

"Aunt Winnie is pretty special, too. Uncle Al's entire life was wrapped up in telling people about Jesus, and Aunt Winnie's still is."

"We prayed."

Still leaning on the headrest, Tony angled toward Kenna. Had he heard her correctly? Had she meant what he thought she meant? "What kind of prayer?" he asked as casually as he could manage.

"To believe. To be forgiven."

Tony released a breath he hadn't been aware he was holding. *Thank You, Jesus. I jumped the gun. I know I did, but thank You.* "I'm glad. That means a lot to me."

"It's all so strange. So new."

"I'm sure it is. We can talk about it more if you want."

"I'd like that. Winnie said she'd help me learn, too. Like we'd get together a couple of times a week while your grandmother naps."

Bless Aunt Winnie. "That's a great idea." Knowing his aunt, the study would be systematic and totally geared to Kenna's knowledge and progress.

"I don't know how this will affect my life. I mean, I'm a nurse, and that hasn't changed."

Tony studied her shadowed face. Why was she even thinking her job should change?

"I love my job. Well, at least when I don't hate it."

He chuckled. "That sounds about right for most adults, I think. I love cooking. Love running my own kitchen, but I'm super aware that it ties up all my time. Most people who're dating go out in the evenings, but I work most of them."

"Most people who're dating also don't live with an old lady who requires twenty-four-hour care."

"There's that, too. But then, most of them don't live in the same house, either. Unless they're... living together." He scratched his neck where a flush had risen. "But I like you a lot, Kenna. I'm willing to try and figure out how to have a relationship with you, even though our situation isn't exactly normal." He held his breath for a few seconds. Why didn't she say something? "How about you?"

Her other hand rested on top of their joined ones. "I'd consider myself the luckiest woman in Bridgeview."

Tony met her gaze in the dim light then stretched toward her. He swept his lips over hers, but that wasn't enough. He rose to his feet and tugged her to standing. The fuzzy blanket dropped back onto the patio chair as he gathered her close and kissed her.

19

*L*ate evenings became Kenna's favorite time of day out on the patio as October stretched on. She brought a pair of snuggly fleece blankets out while she waited for Tony to come home from the restaurant, since nights were much chillier than they'd been. But maybe it was love keeping her warm. How should she know? She'd never felt this with her late husband. Maurice had expected physical intimacy from the beginning, but they'd never achieved emotional intimacy.

Kenna doubted Maurice had even known such a thing existed. She certainly hadn't. Not until these autumn nights, holding hands and talking until the wee hours. And the kissing. She loved the kissing, but she also loved that there was more to this burgeoning relationship.

They talked of childhood dreams. She told him about her father's abuse and suicide. Tony held her while she cried for the first time since bottling away all the emotion for nearly two decades. He told her about growing up in Galena Landing. About working as a dishwasher at The Sizzling

Skillet with a jerk for a boss. By the time he'd been fired for talking back, he'd caught the cooking bug.

What she didn't talk about was Maurice. There wasn't much to say. Marrying him had not been her finest moment, and she still couldn't quite place why she'd run off to Vegas with a man she'd just met. She knew why she'd stayed, though. Quitting wasn't in her nature. She was tougher than that.

"Do you have a job to go back to?" Tony asked.

Kenna grimaced, not that he could likely read her expression in the shadows. "Sort of? I can go back to the geriatrics ward. It's on call, but I can pick up quite a few shifts. It's just..." She let her thoughts drift away.

"Just what?" His voice was gentle.

"The supervisor doesn't like me."

"I'm sorry."

She took a deep breath. "A lot of people don't like me."

"I do. Quite a lot." This time she could hear a smile in his words.

Kenna turned toward him, searching his shadowed face. "Why did it change? Because I know you didn't, at first."

Tony chuckled. "I think we're too much alike."

Too much alike. Did that mean their personalities would keep being a problem between them? "You're not like me at all. People admire you and want to be around you. You're a good boss." She'd spent a couple of more evenings sitting in the back of the kitchen at Antonio's. She'd seen how Tony interacted with his staff, even how he'd corrected some when needed. They respected him. Admired him.

If that had been Kenna's kitchen, everyone would have staged a protest and walked out in one fell swoop. Probably by Day Two.

"It's a lot harder than I thought it would be." Tony leaned his head back, his fingers toying with hers. "More than half my staff is older than me, some by decades. The knowledge I pay their wages mostly keeps them from protesting, but I can tell being ordered around by a young upstart is painful for some. I'm pretty sure that's why some of my earlier hires moved on. I've worked in plenty of restaurants since high school, but the owner-manager was always someone old enough to be respected."

"Age isn't everything."

"Don't I know it? But that's not what we were talking about. You and me, we're both opinionated. We quickly analyze a situation, make a snap decision, and move on. And then we stand by that decision, come what may."

Which about summed up Kenna's marriage to Maurice. Next time she'd be far more cautious. Wait. There wasn't going to be a next time. Hadn't she made a resolution about that? She had.

Then why was she sitting out in the darkness with Tony night after night, holding hands, sharing the depths of her being, kissing him? What did she think this was going to lead to? Because when Marietta was able and fit, Kenna would move back to her apartment, go back to her unfulfilling job, and forget Tony existed.

Only, she'd never forget him. Somehow, in the time she'd known him, she'd fallen for him. Maybe... maybe even tumbled all the way into love.

No! Kenna jerked to her feet and flung Tony's hand away as though it had been a stinging wasp. "I need to go inside."

He surged to his feet and reached for her. "Are you okay?"

She wrapped both arms around her middle and backed

up, causing the deck chair to skitter noisily across the stones. "This... I'm not sure I can do this."

The movements caused the motion sensor light to come on, so the confusion on his face was clearly visible. Confusion and concern. "What did I say? That we're a lot alike? We are, but that isn't a problem. It can work in our favor. We should be able to understand each other more easily that way."

Kenna circled the chair so she could keep some distance between them. "You're not like me. I'm not lovable. I'm mean. I'm harsh."

"Sweetheart."

Her heart hiccupped. He'd never used such a tender word with her before. "You've been so nice to me, making me feel..." Loved. But she couldn't say that out loud. Not when he'd never used that word himself.

"Kenna. I admit I didn't react well to you at first. I didn't know how to cope with someone so—"

"Pushy?"

"I was going to say beautiful. And strong."

"Beautiful?" That's not what the little old men in the wards called it. They called her sexy when they were being polite. Taunting. Sending mixed signals. Not that most of them could have done anything to take advantage of her. They were aged, ill, and bedridden, after all.

"Yes, Kenna. You're beautiful. Inside and out."

"You mean after the crusty."

"I wish I knew what I'd said wrong. I... admire you. Appreciate you."

Kenna didn't want admiration. Not from Tony. She wanted love. Except she didn't, because he was right. She made decisions, and then she stood by them. And she'd decided to remain single for the rest of her life. If it looked long and bleak, that was just too bad. No man was going to truly love her. She could acknowledge the beautiful. She'd worked hard on that, because it was her only natural asset. The only thing that could draw people — men — to her. But then she didn't want the attention it provoked, and the ugly inside gushed out.

Like now.

Hadn't she prayed with Winnie a few weeks ago? Hadn't Jesus promised to make her a new person on the inside? She'd even thought it might be working, but maybe not. Maybe she was stuck with the old Makenna Johnson Hamelin until she landed up in one of those long-term care beds being bathed and fed by a young thing in scrubs and a life outside of work.

She took a long, shuddering breath and backed up a couple of more steps. "I need to go inside. It's late."

"Can we pray together before you go in?" Tony's voice was sweet. Gentle.

Kenna shook her head. "Not tonight."

"I'll pray for you, anyway. Because you are just as important to God as ever. Just as loved."

She fled in the patio door, but just before it snicked shut, she heard Tony's final words. "And to me."

ᗡ ᐧ ᑕ ᐧ

TONY PACED the small space he called home, but it wasn't big enough, so he opened the door to the storage area to give him a longer circuit. Over the past weeks, his uncles and aunts had gone through the majority of the items that Nonna had tucked in there over the years. Family members had taken some of the furniture and artwork, while other pieces had been donated to thrift stores. No one wanted the hassle of running a garage sale. And several truckloads of items deemed worthless had been quietly disposed of.

Nonna had spent a while glaring and making snide comments to everyone around her, but she'd finally admitted that it was a load off her mind. She kept the lacquer box on her dresser, but if she'd seen Kenji since the birthday party, Tony didn't know about it.

Was his personality like his grandmother's? Like him, she didn't suffer fools gladly. She was very opinionated and didn't care who knew her thoughts. Most people liked her and respected her, but some thought she was rude and forceful, not seeing the love in her heart. Even some of Tony's cousins kept their time with Nonna at a minimum.

But what of Kenna? She and Nonna had gotten on well from the beginning. The clash had been between Kenna and him. It had been more than fifty percent his fault, though. He'd antagonized her the first time they'd met. He'd felt so inadequate. His uncles and aunts had pushed him to living with Nonna to keep an eye on her. So she wouldn't be alone all the time. Not three months later, he'd failed utterly. She'd fallen, broken multiple bones, and Tony had been helpless to do a single thing to care for her. And so her kids had hired a nurse to do what Tony could not. They hadn't even consulted him.

Why should they? They were focused on their mamma. They hadn't meant to brush Tony aside. Hadn't meant to impose on his personal space or take advantage of his ability to cook Italian comfort food for a crowd.

But Kenna. He'd said how they were so much alike. He'd thought that was a compliment, but that's not how she'd taken it. His words had triggered something in her. He had to admit, it wasn't the first time he'd said the wrong thing, but he'd thought they were past the shutting-down reaction. He hadn't seen it since she'd become a Christian. Since they'd started their nightly talks on the patio.

Why this time?

He'd meant to carry on and tell her how much she meant to him. That maybe he even loved her. Could he love someone who went into lockdown if she felt threatened? Was it too late to backpedal out of his ever-deepening feelings? Because love didn't play the rollercoaster game. Kisses of promise, long talks, and then all windows shuttered and a *no trespassing* sign on a door slammed in his face.

Tony had promised to pray for her, and he would. But what kind of prayers? The kind where God gave him the right words to soothe her hurts?

No. Her healing had to come from the Lord. It wasn't Tony she needed to turn to when she felt threatened. It was Jesus. Tony couldn't do that for her, but he could do as he'd promised and pray.

And then maybe back off. Be too tired to linger on the patio after work, or possibly find it too cold. Maybe she wouldn't even be waiting outside tomorrow. Maybe this was the beginning of the end for their fledgling relationship. He hadn't even made it formal. They'd been drifting toward more, and it never seemed like the right time to put a label on it. Had that been wrong? Or had it been wisdom?

Tony ran his hands through his hair and pivoted to make another lap. How was he supposed to know? His emotions were in a massive tangle, and it was impossible to know which direction was up. Maybe God had been protecting him from declaring his deepening feelings. Maybe this was how it was supposed to end.

Kenna would still be caring for Nonna for the next few weeks, but they could avoid each other. They'd done that well enough for the first while. Besides, Nonna's ability to care for herself was increasing daily now that the cast was finally off her arm.

Soon Kenna would be gone out of Tony's life. He'd be able to focus on Nonna. On the restaurant.

On his sad and lonely life. Maybe one day before he turned forty, he would meet a woman who could return his love. She'd need to be younger than him so they could have children. He wasn't willing to forego a family forever, but this wasn't the right season for it with the hours he was working. Even at the best of times, a chef's family could suffer from his restaurant hours.

He and Kenna had never talked about kids. The topic was too personal for an undefined relationship, but with the focus she had on nursing, maybe she didn't feel the yearning most women seemed to have. Or maybe his experience was tainted by a large family living in the midst of a neighborhood with piles of babies. Seemed everyone had kids or was expecting soon. It was getting to him more than he'd foreseen.

Maybe he was better off without her.

His head could say that, but his heart protested. Rocky start or not, his heart knew he'd met his match.

Tony dropped on his knees beside his bed and began to pray.

20

*M*arietta pushed her walker in front of her, a determined look on her face.

"You're doing well."

The old woman grunted. "To think I once took mobility for granted. Going to the restroom by myself."

Kenna couldn't blame Marietta for feeling frustrated. It had been nearly three months since the tumble that had changed her life. Of course, no one expected her to rebound like one of her great-grandchildren would have, but there'd been more setbacks than they'd foreseen. Soon, though, she wouldn't need help anymore.

Then Kenna would move back to her apartment, forcing Carol to decide if she was returning to Dave or filing for divorce. She'd keep looking for a better nursing position. This had been a lovely interlude.

Except with Tony.

Especially with Tony. For the first time ever, Kenna'd felt treasured and appreciated. Maybe even loved. But it couldn't keep going. She'd stopped the nighttime talks and kisses. She refused his invitation to the kitchen at Antonio's as well as his food offerings for her and his grandmother. When he came upstairs to visit, she took the opportunity to leave the house or hide in her room.

Yes, she was chicken, but it was for the best. He'd get over her and find someone else to love. Someone who deserved a great guy like him and didn't clash with him constantly.

It would take her longer to recover, but that was okay, because it would serve as a reminder that she'd made up her mind and would stick to it.

Marietta wobbled.

Kenna reached out to steady her. "Easy there. You're doing well."

"I wish you would tell me what happened with Antonio."

It wasn't the first time the topic had surfaced. Kenna shook her head. "He has a bright future ahead of him."

"So do you," mumbled her client.

Nice sentiment. "It's better this way."

Marietta eased herself into a wingback chair. "You have put your trust in Jesus."

Kenna nodded. She'd finished reading the paperback Winnie had given her and moved on to others she recommended.

"Have you prayed about Tony?"

What? Kenna's gaze snapped to Marietta's.

"Or have you made a decision from fear?"

Oh, how she'd like to tell the old lady it was none of her business. It really wasn't. Was it fear, though? Definitely self-protection. Being vulnerable was... well, opening the door to being hurt. Enough pain came to those who cocooned themselves without stepping out there and asking for it. "When Kenji Ito came to visit, why did you tell him no? Was it from fear?"

Marietta studied her face. "No, I do not think so. Kenji does not share the faith that you and I share. That my grandson shares. I am too old, too decrepit to love again, and it seems pointless to hold out that hope."

At least Kenna had diverted the topic. "Maybe he just wanted a friend."

"Perhaps, but I don't think so. Let us say for a moment that you are right, though."

Kenna blinked and focused on the old woman again. "What? Why, if you're sure?"

"I had a great love with Salvador. I lost him much too soon, but we had five wonderful sons together. But the youngest has gone to his reward. Alberto. So unexpected. So much hurt."

"It's been hard for Winnie." It seemed the right thing to say, even though Winnie seemed eager to love again. How could that be?

"It has. She is young to be a widow. As are you. There is much love left to enjoy."

"You would encourage her to marry again?" Kenna couldn't believe it. Wouldn't Al's mother think Winnie should hold his memory close forever? This family was mad. Every one of them, just as Maurice had said.

"My son is gone." Marietta dabbed a tear from her cheeks. "But perhaps you are correct that I fear pain. My body has betrayed me, and the thought of purposefully stepping into any place where pain is possible doesn't seem wise. Perhaps you understand this."

All too well. Kenna looked away.

"So here is what we will do, you and me. We will together pray, si?"

They already prayed together over meals. Sometimes about other things. So how was this different? Kenna studied the older woman. "About what?"

"About being open to the will of our loving Lord and Savior." Marietta nodded toward an arrangement of dried lavender that had appeared on the wall about the same time the fresh bouquets had stopped.

Kenna figured either Jasmine or Winnie was responsible for it, but she'd never asked. There'd been sachets tucked in the linen closet and potpourri in pretty bowls on the bathroom counters. The stuff had infiltrated everywhere. She doubted she'd ever again in her life smell lavender and not remember her time with the Santoro family.

"It is to soothe, si? To keep us from being uptight."

Us? Which made her wonder whether the perpetrators had targeted Kenna or Marietta. Probably both.

"It is like the love of Jesus. He lavishes it on us and asks only that we allow it to permeate our lives. Like yeast in a dough, but sweeter smelling."

"Rising bread smells good." Kenna wished she dared try baking some, but Winnie brought some occasionally. Besides, that was Tony's area. She couldn't compete.

Was that thought being open to Jesus' will? Did God care about her issues with men? With Tony? Sure, he was a very special man, but that was a problem she carried on her own. It wasn't God's issue.

"The Bible speaks of God knowing the very number of hairs on our head," mused Marietta. "Of caring for each sparrow. It also says we should cast all our burdens on Him, because He cares for us. And so we will do that. Together."

Kenna nodded dumbly.

"And then we shall see if you will fix things with my grandson." Marietta stared out the window for a long moment while Kenna held her breath. Then she turned back. "And if I agree to have tea with Kenji Ito, as a friend only. He is a lonely man and needs a friend."

So this wasn't simply a pointed attack on Kenna's tight grip on her life. Mrs. Santoro truly was looking at the wider picture. And if the old woman thought that God cared about such things, even though they seemed utterly selfish, then Kenna would try to wrap her brain around it.

It was a pleasant Monday morning for November. Tony padded into his tiny kitchen and started a coffee in his pressurized moka pot. He'd been home to Galena Landing on his days off last week, and it wouldn't be very adult of him to make the trip a constant habit. He'd left home ten years ago, lived in Seattle and Arcadia Valley and now Bridgeview. He wasn't a kid anymore to hide in his cozy fort under the dining room table when things seemed rough.

But his days off for the past couple of weeks had stretched endlessly since Kenna had closed him out. He'd played some three-on-three with his cousins. He'd helped Logan Dermott assemble an intricate gazebo for a client. Now the family was gearing up for Peter and Sadie's Thanksgiving wedding. Everyone would gather. Tony had made the difficult decision to close on Saturday evening. His staff would work on Thanksgiving itself but have the extra time on the weekend, just so he could attend his cousin's wedding. Was Peter supposed to schedule a morning wedding just because of Tony's life? Of course not.

The coffee burbled through, nearly loud enough to mask the sound of his ringing phone. He reached for it, recognizing Nonna's number. He sighed, hating the situation that kept him from spending time with her. Hating even more that Kenna refused his presence. What was a guy to do?

Besides pray. He was wearing a hole in the carpet by his bed.

"Antonio?"

He smiled at that. It might be the name on his birth certificate, but it wasn't him. It was the chef — the restaurant, even — not the man. "Good morning, Nonna."

"I have need of you today."

Best to be cautious. "Oh?"

"Makenna and I are going to the Nishinomiya Garden in Manito Park."

He grinned as she totally mangled the pronunciation. "How come? The Japanese garden isn't at its best this time of year." Or so he'd assume. He'd only been through once in early spring, and the blossoms had been phenomenal. For one reason or another, he'd never returned. Too busy. Well, not today.

She hesitated. "We meet Kenji Ito."

"Really?" The question escaped in his surprise. "I thought you said there was nothing between you." He poured the coffee into a mug.

"There is not, but he needs a friend. I have another reason to ask you. I want to walk, but I am not so good at it yet. Kenna insists we take the wheelchair in case. But she cannot help me walk while she pushes the empty wheelchair."

Tony's eyebrows rose. As near as he'd been able to figure out, Kenna could do pretty much anything she put her mind to. This might not be the moment to remind Nonna, though. He wracked his brain. "Isn't it a gravel path?"

"I can manage it if you will come."

"Does Kenna know you're asking me?" The question popped out before he had a chance to censor it. He'd been careful not to air their problems to his grandmother. She had such a penchant for meddling he was only amazed she hadn't started before this. Maybe the nighttime patio visits had escaped Nonna's attention. Maybe she hadn't noticed the softer looks they'd exchanged for a time.

Nah, Nonna was ever the matchmaker. She missed nothing.

"She knows."

And Kenna was willing? That put a different spin on it. His heart leaped. "In that case, sure, I'd love to. When and where?"

Kenna could hardly blame Tony for driving over in his own car, but didn't that just reveal how little he trusted spending time with her? She deserved that after the past couple of weeks.

He offered her a quick smile but focused on helping his grandmother out of the car while Kenna hauled the wheelchair out of the hatchback and unfolded it.

An older vehicle in impeccable condition pulled up beside them, and Kenji Ito got out. He looked stately in a gray coat and a bowler hat, and his gaze slid immediately to Marietta.

Great. Four people going on this outing, and every one of them nervous. This should be a ton of fun.

The elderly man offered his arm to Marietta, and she took it. They ambled toward the pergola that marked the entrance.

Now what? Kenna looked between the walker and the wheelchair. She and Tony would look ridiculous following the older couple pushing the mobility accessories.

"There are quite a few benches." Tony shoved his hands in his jeans pockets. "I vote I run back and get one of these things if we need it."

Kenna didn't want to look at him, but now that he'd spoken, she couldn't tear her gaze away. He looked good in those jeans and a slim down jacket. She longed to smooth the curls by his ears. The man needed a haircut since she'd last had that right.

But was it a right? Or had she taken advantage of him, pouncing on him every night as he came home from work, keeping him up so he couldn't get enough sleep? Not that he looked rested now, either. There were shadows under his eyes.

She had them, too, but hopefully she'd applied enough makeup he wouldn't be able to tell. "Sounds like a plan." She refolded the wheelchair, but Tony took it from her before she could lift it and deposited it in the vehicle.

Kenna stepped out of the way and pushed her hands into her coat pockets as he closed the back. She could avoid this awkwardness by hurrying to catch up with Marietta and Kenji — not that they'd gotten very far — but she'd promised her client to do her best to make amends. "Um, how are you doing?"

Tony's blue eyes darkened as he glanced at her. "Okay, ish. How about you?"

Wow, that had been noncommittal. Which she totally deserved. "I'm planning to move out right after Thanksgiving. Maybe even that weekend, since your parents will be staying with your grandmother."

He gave a curt nod and headed toward the gate. "That's what you've wanted all along."

"Not all along."

She kept her voice soft, but he'd heard her. She could tell by the hesitation in his step, but he carried on. He stepped up beside Marietta and Kenji, who'd paused to peer into the koi pond.

Kenna stared after him, feeling every bit the outsider she was. Marietta had done this more for Kenna's sake than her own, but look at her, hand tucked in the crook of Kenji's arm, sharing a moment, while Tony had already rejected Kenna... just as she'd done to him. Walked away while he pleaded with her to stay.

She hadn't begged yet. Begging didn't come easy. A woman had her pride. But it was more than that. She didn't want him to know how needy she was, but how could they have a relationship if she wasn't honest with him? She'd prided herself all her life on making decisions and following through, but what if her decision had been wrong? What if they could be reversed? She'd never allowed for that.

But she'd been wrong to push Tony aside when he'd called her sweetheart. It hadn't been an insult when he said they were alike. Being like him could never be mockery. He was wonderful. Kind. Gentle. Awesome.

Okay, sure, he'd had his crusty moments, as had she. But

now she had this moment to humble herself and admit vulnerability. And then he'd stick to his earlier decision, of course, and that would be the end of anything that might have been.

Was it even worth trying when the outcome was already set?

Love conquers all.

Kenna gathered her courage around her like a cloak and stepped into the Japanese garden.

21

*W*hy had Nonna invited him on this outing? She didn't need him, that was obvious. She kept her hand tucked at Kenji's elbow, and the two of them ambled so slowly down the hard-packed path along Kiri Pond that they'd never complete the circuit before dark. They'd barely crested the iconic bridge, let alone reached the first bench to take a rest.

Tony stiffened as Kenna came up beside him. Hadn't he wanted to talk to her? But now that the moment was here and she seemed amenable, accusations and frustration whirled around in his mind. It would be all too easy to say the wrong thing and not have a clue what it was. Again.

"I'm sorry, Tony."

He inhaled slowly before glancing at the woman beside him. She was beautiful as always, her blond hair curling past her shoulders, her gray eyes bordering on purple as she met his gaze. Was that a reflection from her down coat the way the arched bridge lay mirrored in the still pond, with Nonna and Kenji looking over the edge?

His heart hiccupped. He should be over Kenna. Liking her at all had crept past his strong barriers. Becoming a friend — then falling in love — had been way more than he bargained for. Then to be shut out cold two weeks ago... what was he supposed to do with that?

"For what?" His question covered the scope of his thoughts, whatever direction she chose to take it, if any at all.

"I'm not really good with change. You said it yourself. You reminded me."

Tony wracked his brain through the conversation that night. Parts of it were etched in his memory. Other parts, not so much. "I think it was a compliment." Hadn't it been about her making a decision and sticking to it? That was commendable, wasn't it?

"It reminded me of a promise I'd made to myself. Something I'd been pushing aside."

He waited, hands shoved deep into his jeans' pockets, his gaze fixed on his grandmother not six feet away. She said something quietly to her companion, who offered a small smile.

When Kenna didn't elaborate, Tony glanced at her again. "What was that?"

"After Maurice died, I promised myself that I'd never marry again. Never risk falling in love again."

"Did you love him?"

She shrugged. "In some ways, I guess I did. It wasn't all bad. But when I see other couples' relationships, like Jasmine and Nathan even, I know we only had the shell of a marriage. Maurice cared far more about his own comfort than he did for me."

Tony didn't want to think about what it must have been

like. He'd never met the man, only heard stories. But if he were ever to understand Kenna, ever move forward with her, he'd need to wrap his head around her past. Huh. Just because she was talking didn't mean they were moving forward. Didn't mean he wanted to expose himself to her rejection again.

"I told myself I didn't need anyone else. I could take care of myself. I don't need much, just enough to keep body and soul together. Nursing provides enough income for basic living expenses. And it enables me to care for others just enough to satisfy that part of me, but without caring too deeply. Too personally."

"You've been hurt." Her stories of her father's death. Her mother's rejection. Her marriage to Maurice. No wonder her barriers were as scalable as Mount Rainier or Denali... and yet those had been climbed by men and women trained and dedicated. Was Tony up to the task? Seriously?

"It's been my shield."

He nodded.

"But your grandmother reminded me that by thinking and living that way, I'm not trusting Jesus. I opened my heart to Him but then made sure He wasn't one of the many to spread pain in my life. How could I trust Him?" Her voice broke slightly. "When I can't trust anyone but myself?"

It hadn't been about him all along. Not at the core, but that didn't keep his heart safe. Wait. Was he doing what she was doing? Shifting blame so he didn't have to face his own shortfalls? Protecting himself at all cost?

Tony stopped in the path and looked at Kenna. Really looked. Past her beauty, into the vulnerable depths her eyes revealed. This wasn't a show put on for his benefit. Her struggles were deep and real... and not something he was equipped to deal with.

People were hungry? Great. He could solve that with delectable Italian food. People needed a bit of pampering? The decor in the alcoves and rooftop at Antonio's had been created with that special experience in mind. Hurting people needed prayer? He could do that, too, with or without the Thursday morning prayer group. He didn't need to get deeply involved in anyone's problems, simply make things better for a little while or refer them to an expert.

But Kenna needed more, and he might be the only one to provide it. He might be the only one who knew her enough.

Loved her enough.

How could he not meet her halfway when she'd opened up and shown her vulnerability?

Tony took a step closer, and she turned to face him. He yearned to take her in his arms and kiss her fears away, but that wouldn't solve the heart of her problem. Only God could meet here there, so Tony kept his hands firmly wedged in his pockets.

"Letting go of things — letting God handle them — that's a core growth area for believers. You're not the only one who struggles there."

Kenna sucked in her bottom lip as she searched his face.

He forced himself to keep his focus on her eyes.

"Do you?" she asked softly.

"Struggle with letting God manage my life? So much." Clarity sifted over him, so overwhelming he glanced at the sky to see if the sun had just appeared from behind a cloud. But there were no clouds. No shadows.

"How do you do it?"

"It's a process that will likely take my entire life. It's a decision every day, sometimes dozens of times. It's a matter of spending time in God's word, getting to know Him, to trust Him. And then, when I mess up — and I do, often — it's a matter of asking His forgiveness and starting over with the decisions of trust."

"It never gets easier?"

Tony considered the question. She didn't deserve a slap-dash, pious reply. "It does get easier, but only as much as I keep my eyes focused on Jesus. If I start living for myself, I trip and fall pretty quickly. We're never going to be perfect on this earth, but that doesn't mean we shouldn't strive to become the best version of ourselves we can be."

"I guess I somehow thought Jesus would change every-thing. Like flipping a switch."

"Sounds like that would be helpful, doesn't it? But growth isn't magic. It's a process." He hesitated, searching her eyes. "And sometimes we need help. I know you've been meeting with my aunt Winnie, and she's great, but you might want to consider some appointments with Juanita Ramirez, Pastor Tomas's wife. She's a credentialed coun-selor, and I think she could help you work through things."

Kenna nodded slowly and sighed. "You're right. I need a shrink."

"That's not what I said," Tony said softly. "But if you do, that's okay, too. You're worth it."

Her gaze jumped to his and locked.

"And to answer your original question, I forgive you. Will you forgive me?"

A shout from across the small pond caught his attention. Kenji waved both arms, obviously distraught.

And Nonna slumped on a bench, grasping at her throat.

ONE GLANCE, and Kenna broke into a record-breaking hundred-yard dash. Down the path, over the bridge, around the other side.

How could she have let the elderly couple get so far away from her? She was responsible for Marietta! Nothing could happen to her on Kenna's watch.

"What happened?" she yelled as she sprinted closer. But it was obvious the old woman was choking.

"I gave her a cookie, and she laughed while she took a bite."

Kenna heard the words dimly as she braced Marietta with her left arm and delivered a sharp blow between the shoulder blades with her right hand. Again. Again.

But nothing changed. The old woman was a dead weight against Kenna's arm, not even struggling. Conscious, but not breathing.

Kenna shifted to abdominal thrusts. Always dangerous, especially on someone fragile, but not as dangerous as not breathing for four minutes. They might have already lost one quarter of that precious time.

She wrapped her arms around Marietta with a fist just below the rib cage. Then she pulled in and up, hard and fast.

Marietta coughed and expelled a small object then slumped more heavily against Kenna's grip.

"Help me lay her down!"

Instantly Tony was at her side. Together they laid his grandmother beside the path.

"Is she okay?"

Kenna glanced up to see Kenji wringing his hands, worry marring his handsome features.

"I think so, but we need to get her to the hospital to be checked."

Marietta was breathing. That was the most important thing at the moment.

Kenna willed her adrenaline to subside. She'd done what she could. She'd done enough. But had she done *too* much? She'd felt those barely healed ribs give way, but did she need to mention that right now? Could they manage with the wheelchair, or should she call an ambulance?

"I'll get the wheelchair, but I need your keys." Tony held out his hand.

Kenna hooked them out of her purse, willing to let him make the decision... not that he was the expert here, nor the one who had all the information.

Kenji lowered himself awkwardly beside Marietta. "I am so sorry. I would never forgive myself if something happened to you."

Marietta turned her head a little, wincing, and opened her eyes to look at the man. "Not your fault," she whispered.

That wince. Kenna knew. Oh, man. What had she done?

⌒ ⸜ ⸝

"Kenna! What brings you here?" The emergency room nurse faced her across the gurney.

"My client. She was choking. Thumps between the

shoulder blades did not dislodge the object, so I moved to abdominal thrusts. That did dispel the blockage, but..."

She said more, but her voice quieted, and Tony couldn't quite catch her words from where he stood with Kenji. Not that it mattered. He'd been present. He'd seen what happened as much as she had.

"I'll talk to the doctor, but I'm sure we'll get her in for a chest X-ray shortly."

A chest X-ray? Why? To see if there were more particles stuck? Maybe that was why. Nonna certainly hadn't rebounded the way other near-choking victims had in Tony's limited experience. That guy in the restaurant a few weeks ago had walked out, laughing and talking and leaving a generous tip.

Nonna definitely wasn't up for that.

Kenji shuffled beside Tony. "Is she all right?"

"I think so." Or, at least, he'd thought so before their arrival at Deaconess. He'd followed Kenna's car with Kenji behind him like they were in some kind of parade. Having Nonna checked out seemed like a wise idea then, but only a precaution. Now? He wasn't so sure.

A doctor in scrubs consulted with Kenna and the other nurse then made a note on her tablet. An orderly whisked Nonna away.

If it weren't for Kenji, Tony would have been in the thick of the discussions and decisions. It chafed him not to be, but Kenna was far more able to handle things in this environment than he was, and someone needed to stay with Kenji Ito. Though why he felt responsible for the old man, who knew?

The other nurse laughed at something Kenna said.

So things with Nonna couldn't be as dire as Tony had begun to dread. Right?

She lightly punched Kenna's shoulder, turning so her voice carried. "That's one way to make sure you're needed longer! I get to keep your apartment through Christmas, right?"

What on earth? Tony frowned. His pulse sped to a thundering roar, and he took a step closer.

Kenna glanced his way. Her eyes widened and her hand clapped over her mouth.

Oh, she realized he'd overheard her friend, had she? The nerve of her — the nerve of them both.

Tony shot poison darts from his eyes. He'd get to the bottom of this. For sure. But not when he was likely to make a fool of himself in public. He pivoted, marched out the sliding glass doors, and hung a tight right.

What on earth had the other nurse meant? Why did Kenna look so guilty? Had she been playing Tony all along?

22

*H*e hasn't talked to me since Monday." Kenna curled her feet under her on her own sofa and faced Carol. "On Tuesday, Grace Santoro — one of my client's daughters-in-law — kindly told me I could have Thanksgiving weekend off since Tony's parents would be staying at the house for a few days, and his mom is a long-term care aide. I'm sure Tony put his aunt up to it."

Carol looked down, her hands covering her face for a long moment. "I can't tell you how sorry I am for joking about that."

Kenna set her face and stared out the window at the late November sky. Gray, like her heart. Like everything in her life. "You didn't know."

Man, she wanted to hold this against Carol forever. How dare the other woman let something so flippant slip from her lips? And Tony had only overheard the incriminating part, obviously assuming Carol had meant Kenna would do anything to keep her cushy job in Mrs. Santoro's house. But

Carol knew about Tony, just enough that the tease was about giving Kenna longer to regroup that romance.

Fat chance of that happening now. Tony was as quick to anger and lash out as Kenna was. And he was angry now, no doubt about it.

Two could play that game. If he didn't trust her, she didn't want him anyway.

Isn't it a good thing that's not how God treated me?

Kenna closed her eyes as tears threatened to surge. She'd spent a few days holding her frustration and anger like a shield. The situation proved she couldn't trust anyone. She'd let her guard down over the past weeks with Tony, but this was a solid warning that she was better off alone.

I will never leave you or forsake you.

That bit was from the Bible and had been in one of the books Winnie shared. Kenna wasn't alone anymore, but she felt lonelier than ever. Than ever? Even when Dad killed himself? Even during her marriage to Maurice?

No. Not that alone.

"Carol, I — do you know anything about God?"

"About... God?"

Kenna swiped an errant tear away and looked at her friend. The friend she barely knew for all they'd worked together for nearly three years, because Kenna kept to herself. It was time to change that. She might never remarry, as she'd pledged herself, but it was too late to say she'd never fall in love again. Tony had her heart, whether he wanted it or not.

Either way, though, her experience with Jesus had been real, and she'd definitely shoved it aside in the past few days as much as Tony had blocked her out.

"I'm sure you don't know Winnie Santoro, but she's

another of my client's daughters-in-law. She lost her husband a couple of years ago when a drunk driver T-boned his truck."

"Alberto Santoro?"

Kenna blinked her friend into focus. "Yes. You do know her?"

"I was working ICU when he was brought in. Man, that family." Carol shook her head, eyes lost in thought. "The waiting room was packed for days with people having prayer meetings for him. They really stood out in my mind because of all the support and, well, optimism. Not just hoping he'd come out of the coma, but something deeper."

"They have peace because of their hope in God."

Carol looked at Kenna. "Yeah, that sounds about like what I remember. Winnie... she talked to me about Jesus. There she was with her husband hooked up to machines, but she was the one giving out comfort to staff. I've never seen anything like it."

"That sure sounds like Winnie. She's been talking to me about Jesus, too. And..." Kenna took a deep breath. "I wanted what she has."

"I don't blame you. It sounded mighty appealing in that moment."

"So I prayed. And I've been doing a lot of reading."

"Well." Carol angled her head and studied Kenna. "I wondered what this was all about. Because the coworker I knew never seemed to want to be real friends." Her eyebrows rose. "Are you trying to save my soul now?"

"What? No. I'm sorry about being so unfriendly. I know I wasn't... nice. I've spent my entire life defending myself from one thing or another, but that's no excuse. The results were just what I'd worked for. No one was close, so no one could hurt me. But being alone is painful, too, and I've discovered there's more joy in taking a chance on people even if I get hurt."

"Okay... even Tony?"

Kenna swallowed. "Maybe? Because I honestly didn't think I had the capacity to love someone. Like, at all. But maybe I do."

Carol surged to her feet. "And then I came along and blew it for you. He misunderstood, but I shouldn't have teased you anyway. I feel horrible."

"It's okay." And somehow, it was becoming so. The reminder of Winnie's strong faith, the reading Kenna had done, Pastor Tomas's sermons, the talks with Marietta and Tony... yes, things looked bad now, but it wasn't the end. Carol was right in one way. Kenna did have a longer time-frame to make amends. Maybe Tony wouldn't be open to it. She'd have to accept that if it's what happened. Either way, she'd been ignoring the tiny seedlings of faith that had sprouted a while back. She wasn't going to do that anymore.

Her friend turned from the window, studying her. "Thanks. Though I don't get it. You should be kicking me out of the apartment and never talking to me again."

"The old Makenna would have." She chuckled, her heart growing a tiny bit lighter.

"She would have." Carol managed a smile. "And I'm honestly not sure what I would have done if you did. Where I'd go. Dave and I are on such different pages, I don't know if we can ever make things work."

"Do you want to?"

"Yeah, I do. He says he does, too, but we still fight about the same stuff. He figures I should be the one who changes, but have you seen his bad habits?"

"At the risk of sounding like someone who's only out to save your soul, maybe you need a different counselor. I'm just starting to see Juanita Ramirez, but she and her husband, Tomas, do marriage counseling together. Fair warning — he's a pastor."

"Maybe. I don't know. The person we're seeing doesn't seem to offer much constructive help. She's more about listening to us try to hash things out without giving super helpful advice."

"I'll give you Juanita's contact info if you want it."

"Yeah, maybe." Carol huffed a long breath and turned back to the window. "Part of it is Dave says he wants kids, but I don't want to give up my job to stay home with little rug-rats. I'm sure it would have its meaningful moments, but..."

"I only wish I could have kids."

"What? I thought you'd understand. You were married for how long? And never had kids."

Kenna braced herself. The old her would never have talked about this, but the new one knew better. "I had a hysterectomy when I was a teen. At least it got all the cancer."

Carol's eyes widened. "I never knew. I'm sorry. Look at me being all insensitive again."

And that was another elephant in the room. She'd never told Tony. Obviously, she needed to pin the man down — possibly literally — and give him all the information. Then, when he turned away one last time, she'd know she really tried.

Starting with prayer. And more counsel from Juanita.

"IT'S SO BEAUTIFUL," Gina whispered as Peter and Sadie lit a unity candle at the close of their wedding ceremony. She sat between her husband and Tony, Ethan on his dad's lap, trying to see, and three-year-old Emma curled against Tony.

Tony guessed it was a nice wedding. He'd been to a ton of them in the past couple of years. His friends and cousins were dropping like flies, and they all seemed mighty happy about it. For a few weeks, he'd experienced the stirrings of love himself, setting aside the fact that he was far too busy to invest in a relationship right now. He'd been swept away with late-night talks and kisses in the moonlight. Sure, he'd known Kenna was volatile. God only knew he'd had enough warnings on that front, but he'd brushed them aside as though he alone could see and understand the real woman beneath the crusty exterior.

He'd truly thought he was succeeding, but the past couple of weeks had brought his house of cards crashing down.

Tony glanced at his sister, her lips parted and her eyes shining as Pastor Tomas announced Mr. and Mrs. Peter and Sadie Santoro. He leaned closer. "Can we talk later?"

Gina looked up at him, eyebrows rising. "Sure? I mean, we're staying at Fran and Tad's, and Fran and I need a good girl chat, but you're my baby brother, and I'm sure I can sneak five minutes for you. After the kids are in bed."

"I might need more than five minutes."

She grinned and nudged her shoulder against his. "I'll see to it you get them."

Tony nodded and bided his time through the receiving line and the reception. He noticed how the best man's eyes stayed on his girlfriend rather than on the maid of honor at his side. If Tony didn't miss his guess, Alex was going to pop the question to Marley any day now. He'd try to be happy for them.

Nonna looked mighty tired as she sat in her wheelchair over against the far wall during the dancing. The doctor had prescribed extra-strength painkillers to get her through this day — those re-injured ribs kept her very uncomfortable.

Maybe he should take her home, only he didn't know how to be the one to put her to bed. Tony looked around for his mom. Maybe she could slip out long enough to help with Nonna, and then Tony could stay with her while Mom came back for the rest of the reception. He was kind of over being upbeat and happy for everyone.

Cheering, clapping, and whistling from over by the entrance caught his attention. He peered in that direction, too wrapped in his bubble of inertia to figure out what was happening.

His cousin Dafne settled into the vacant chair beside him. "Alex just proposed, and Marley said yes! Isn't that exciting?"

Tony pushed out a smile. "That's great!" Of course, she said yes. Alex would never have risked a public proposal if he hadn't been completely certain of that. Santoro men were no fools.

Except maybe him.

He eyed his cousin. "How are you doing? I haven't seen you lately. Who's got Gavin tonight?" Dafne, a single mom to a two-year-old, had just turned nineteen.

"I hired a sitter. One of my friends from college." She offered a soft smile as she sighed. "We're good. Getting through one day at a time. One prayer at a time. You?"

That there was wisdom. "Same."

"Did you hear Bren and Rob are expecting again?"

Daf had run away as a newly expectant teen and wound up with their cousin Rob's then-girlfriend in Montana, so she knew Bren better than most of the rest of the clan. "Hadn't heard. Good for them."

And he mostly meant it. Rob was one of the few cousins who'd left Spokane, though both Basil and Dominic currently lived in Seattle. Dom was only there for med school, though, claiming he'd return when he finished his training. Only he'd brought his girlfriend home for the weekend to meet his mom, so who knew whether that rumor was true or not.

Everyone was moving on except him. But that wasn't true. Wasn't he the owner of an up-and-coming popular restaurant? Well, he and his uncles, who'd invested in the building and the major renovation it had taken to bring it up to their joint vision. No, Tony was gloomy tonight only because of his single status. He'd gone and fallen for the wrong woman at the wrong time. Now he got to reap the consequences of letting his heart get ahead of him.

Gina sat down across the table. "Fran's taking her kids and mine home to bed. Mom gave me the lowdown on getting Nonna settled for the night, so how about you and I do that?"

"Sounds good." Tony rose and looked down at Dafne. "Good to see you here. Take care."

"You, too." She bounced up and darted across the community center to her sister, Ava.

Gina watched her go with a smile. "That girl's got energy."

"She does. She makes me feel old."

"Not as old as Nonna, I hope. Let's go."

23

*K*enna slid into the back pew on Sunday morning with Carol at her side. Two months ago, she'd have laughed herself silly if anyone suggested she'd come to church voluntarily, let alone bringing a friend, yet here she was. And she actually had a friend to bring.

The Santoro clan filled more of the sanctuary than usual, since the out-of-towners who'd come for Peter and Sadie's wedding yesterday had stayed over. Kenna's gaze found the back of Tony's head instantly, even though it didn't look that different from most of the Santoro guys in his generation. She knew those dark strands — she'd tangled her fingers in them a dozen times.

Once again, his little niece snuggled on his lap where he sat between his sister and his mom, with Marietta's wheelchair on the end beside the center aisle.

Kenna relaxed just a touch seeing her client there. At least the elderly woman wasn't set back too much by Monday's incident.

Not too surprisingly, Pastor Tomas's message today was

on having an attitude of gratitude. Kenna soaked up the words, feeling her heart soften and turn toward the Savior she'd met so recently. Yes, she needed to set aside her hurts and entitlements and shields, and allow herself to find joy in the moments she had.

The service drew to a close, and temptation was strong to sneak out as quietly as she'd come in, but no. She was going to introduce Carol to Juanita. She was going to say hello to Mrs. Santoro and maybe a few others. She'd always faced things head on, and today would be no exception. That was a good part of her personality. The attitude behind it was the part that needed adjusting.

The congregation rose for the benediction. At the amen, Tony turned, still holding the little girl.

Everything else faded out as they stared at each other across the crowded space. She might believe he could forgive her for breaking his grandmother's ribs — after all, she'd saved the old lady's life — but that child in his arms... She needed to talk about children, too, and that would be the deal breaker for sure. Better sooner than later.

The final severing of their tenuous relationship was going to hurt like nothing else in her life ever had, and she was no stranger to pain. But this time, she had a few friends and the greatest friend of all, Jesus. She'd survive this. She would.

The little girl squeezed Tony's cheeks together so tightly his face changed shape. Then she smooched him and giggled. Tony looked down at the child and blew a raspberry on her neck.

The man needed to be a dad. He'd be such a good one. There'd be no way he'd settle for a half-woman like Kenna.

At least she knew that going into their final talks before

she moved out. The promotion she'd been hoping for had gone to someone else, so she'd be back on the floor soon, waiting for another opportunity. One would come, sooner or later.

Carol's elbow in her ribs brought her back to the moment as Juanita wended her way toward them.

"Kenna! Good to see you. We still on for Tuesday?"

"Definitely. And I'd like you to meet my friend Carol. She's looking for someone to talk to about her marriage."

"I'd love to do that." Juanita gave a warm smile as she shook Carol's hand. "I'm Juanita Ramirez. My husband is the pastor here at Bridgeview Bible, but you don't have to be a member to book an appointment. I think I have an opening Wednesday morning. Are you free to chat then for a bit and we can see if we're a good fit?"

"No, I work Wednesday. I'm an ER nurse at Deaconess."

"If you've got a minute now, we can compare your schedule to mine in the admin wing over there." Juanita pointed out an exit off to the side. "Or you can give the office a call when it's convenient for you."

"I've got a few minutes right now. If that's okay with you, Kenna?"

"Sure. I'll wait." She watched the two women cross the rapidly emptying space before realizing it was only Santoros left, a few of them gathered around their matriarch. Tony had set his niece down, and she now tried to guide Gavin around people. She wasn't enough bigger than him to have much impact.

But Tony came toward her, those blue eyes intent on her. "Kenna? I need to apologize."

He what? Her head swam. It was she who'd wronged him, not the other way around.

"I jumped to conclusions, just after telling you I'd forgiven you. I didn't give you a chance to explain. I'm sorry."

She opened her mouth and closed it again, while her dratted eyes filled with leaky emotions. "There's nothing to forgive, but we do need to talk."

"Can I take you to lunch somewhere? I have to be at Antonio's by three-thirty, but I'm yours until then."

That was truer than he suspected. After that, any slight claim she'd had would be gone, but she'd be strong. She needed to do what was right. Kenna took a deep breath. "But your family is here. Don't they want to spend time with you?"

Tony shrugged. "Galena Landing is only a couple of hours' drive. I see them fairly often." He looked in her eyes. "Today I need to sort things out with you. You're more important."

She'd never been more important than anything before. She'd savor it, though it wouldn't last. One last beautiful memory of Tony. "Okay. I need to give Carol a ride back to the apartment. I can meet you somewhere."

∂–ᶜ ᶜ

WAS it a date if he didn't pick her up at the door? He and Kenna hadn't really been on an official date, since most of their relationship had involved talking on the back patio or her watching him work in the Antonio's kitchen. If today went well, he'd step up his game a notch, for sure.

But she'd looked away, all teary-eyed, when she told him they needed to talk, and that ensured he didn't feel too secure yet.

Now he waited in a booth at Morley's, watching the parking lot for her car, hoping she wouldn't stand him up. No, there she was, zipping into a parking spot. When she stepped out, he could see she'd changed her clothes from the pretty dress and pumps she'd worn to church, to striped leggings and a solid purple tunic. He grinned at the purple slip-ons and her matching giant handbag. This woman loved her shoes... even soft ones without swanky heels. Loved her clothes and accessories.

She was gorgeous. He'd been turned off by that at first, thinking she was all about superficiality, but not anymore. Her beauty was natural, and the clothing and the way she carried herself were her defense. She was much softer and more approachable than she'd been when they'd first met more than three months ago.

The server led her to the booth, and Tony stood while she slipped in across from him before resuming his own seat. "You look terrific."

"Thanks." Her gaze flitted to his then away. "You, too."

"Can I get you something to drink? Or are you ready to order?"

Right. The server. "Cheeseburger platter and unsweet iced tea, please."

Kenna glanced at the menu. "Um, chicken Caesar? And a ginger ale, please."

The server nodded and gathered the menus.

Kenna folded her hands on the table for about two seconds before unclasping them and unwrapping the silverware. Then she began systematically tearing the paper napkin into tiny pieces.

"What's wrong, sweetheart?" He hated to prod her, but she was the one who'd said they needed to talk.

She glanced at him again, tears in her eyes.

Tony reached for her hands, but she pulled them into her lap. At least she was looking at him now.

"I can't have kids," she blurted out. Then she jerked to her feet and grabbed her purse. "I should probably leave. Coming here was a mistake."

Tony reeled. Of all the things he'd expected her to discuss, this was not one of them. "Kenna!" He stood and reached for her, but she dodged aside, holding up her monster bag between them.

"You're so good with little ones. Your niece adores you. You need someone in your life who's... whole."

If he let her go now, it was over for sure. He couldn't do that, but he definitely needed a moment to process. "Sweetheart, please sit down. Tell me about it." Was that why she and Maurice had never had a family? He didn't want to think about her previous marriage.

His mind swam. His body felt like it was doing the same. The only anchor was the lock he had on Kenna's gray eyes with their hint of lavender from the purple tunic she wore. Even the thought of lavender gave him a second anchor. Then he remembered to pray. *God, help me. Help us. I don't know what to do, what to say.*

"Please, Kenna. We're here for lunch and to really talk to each other. Let's make sure we do that."

"Are you certain?"

He was so not sure, but he nodded, anyway. There were still as many chances as he needed to back out, but this was the only gateway to move forward. That knowledge pushed to the front. "I'm sure."

Kenna took a deep, shuddering breath, and slid into the booth.

The server appeared with their drinks. "You aren't going to run out on me, are you?" He looked from one to the other.

"No. We're staying." Tony took his seat. "Aren't we, sweetheart?" For some reason, he knew he needed to keep using that endearment. She reacted to it every time. Maybe she didn't believe him. He wasn't sure he believed himself. Again, he pushed that thought aside. He might be the king of snap judgments, but this wasn't a situation that would benefit from it.

The server nodded and moved on to the next booth.

Kenna bit her lip as she looked across the table to him. "I had cancer when I was a teenager. They got it all, but they had to remove my entire reproductive system."

Tony reached for her hands, and this time she let him. "I'm so sorry. That must have been incredibly hard."

"I was fifteen. Barely recuperated from surgery when my dad killed himself."

He winced. But man, that explained a lot. "That's more than any kid should have to bear."

Kenna licked her lips and looked out the window, her hands trembling under his. "I had no one to turn to. Nothing."

He couldn't stand the distance between them. A second later, he slid onto the bench beside her and wrapped his arm across her shoulders. "Hey, I'm here now."

"For how long?" Her whisper was as soft as her shoulders were firm.

"As long as you need me to be." Whether that was five minutes or a lifetime. But he seriously needed to think and pray about that. He couldn't pledge forever love — yes, love — without knowing this was God's best for both of them.

He needed to mourn the family that would never be, but he had to do that on his own time, later. God would show him. Would comfort him. Would give him Elkanah's love for his wife Hannah like in the Old Testament. *Don't I mean more to you than ten sons?*

For now, he wrapped his arms around Kenna until she leaned into him, accepting his support. For now, this was all they both needed.

24

*T*he buffet worked out well then?" Kenna glanced across the car at Tony. Only snow-covered darkness loomed out the window beyond him, but she wasn't concerned about that. She was with Tony, it was Christmas Eve, and they were headed to his parents' home in Galena Landing, Idaho. What more could she want?

"Amazingly. Hopefully it will become an annual tradition. Maybe on the Fourth of July, too. Any holidays where no one wants to eat out in the evening, and my staff doesn't want to work late."

She loved watching his eyes light up when he talked about his restaurant.

"Turns out we had food critics visiting today. They let Dixie know as they were leaving. Hopefully the decent tip they left was indicative of their review."

"That's wonderful. From the culinary guild?"

"They didn't say." His hands flexed on the wheel. "The award doesn't matter."

"Sure, it does."

"No. I don't need the guild to tell me Antonio's is the best new restaurant that opened in Spokane in the past year. Our guests tell me with their reservations and their wallets. The award would be the cherry on top, I'm not gonna lie. But, in the grand scheme of things, it really doesn't matter."

Kenna couldn't resist. "What matters?"

He shot a grin across the car. "You, sweetheart. You and me and Jesus."

She'd reach for his hand across the console, but the two-lane highway was covered with more slush the further north they drove. He needed to keep his focus on the road.

"How was *your* shift?"

Kenna had just come off four straight twelve-hour nights at her new job at the long-term care home. She'd caught a nap while waiting for Antonio's to close and Tony to swing by the apartment to pick her up. "Long, but thankfully quiet. The old man with the flu was finally feeling better and had a decent sleep."

"That's good. You still like your new job better?"

"Yeah. Except I miss working with Carol. But she's back with Dave and they're trying for a baby..." Man, that was still hard to think about.

"I hope it works out for them. They seem like a decent couple."

She and Tony had gone out for dinner with Carol and Dave a couple of times when everyone's time off had coincided. The guys had hit it off. "Are you sure your parents are okay with me intruding on your family Christmas?"

Tony gave her another grin. "I'm not sure how many ways I have to tell you that Mom's thrilled. And that you're not intruding."

"Does she know she'll never get any grandkids out of me?" The words spilled out, louder than she'd intended in the quietness.

This time, Tony's hand sought hers across the car. "She knows, sweetheart. She knows."

"And she wants me anyway?"

"She wants you anyway." He squeezed her fingers then grasped the steering wheel with both hands again. "As do I."

"I still have a hard time believing that. Someday, you'll regret—"

"Makenna Marie."

She swallowed hard at his tender tone. "What?"

"I love you. The rest of it is up to God. There's always adoption. If we had more time in Galena Landing, I'd take you to meet my friends at Green Acres Farm. Six families live there, including Claire and Noel. I told you about Claire, the chef who took mouthy teenage me under her wing?"

Kenna nodded, eyes still teary at the declaration of love.

"Another couple that lives there, Sierra and Gabe, couldn't get pregnant, but they've adopted four kids. The oldest is about seven now. And you know what? They're a great family. It doesn't matter how their kids came."

"Adoption isn't always easy. Sometimes people wait for a lot of years, and not everyone gets chosen." She took a deep breath. "What if we can't adopt?"

"Then we'll still be fine."

Tony seemed determined to be optimistic. Somehow, deep inside, Kenna wasn't quite that sure. They'd talked about the situation several times since Thanksgiving, but her insecurities always cropped up again, no matter how many times Tony assured her it didn't matter.

It did matter.

And she was going to see the evidence all over again with his nephew and niece when they arrived.

⁓

THEY'D BEEN to the Christmas Eve service at the church his parents attended, and now Kenna was settled on the love seat reading a nativity story to Ethan and Emma. Tony entered the kitchen to find his sister. "Thanks for making her feel so welcome."

"Why wouldn't I?" Gina poked his arm. "I've been waiting for years for my baby brother to meet his match and fall in love."

He'd done that, for sure. Hook, line, and sinker. "She's still worried that I'll be sorry after a while when we don't have kids."

Gina's eyebrows rose. "You guys are talking pretty seriously for having only known each other four months."

"This thing about her cancer pushed us a little, honestly, but I don't regret it. We're not nineteen."

"She's five years older than you are."

"So?" Tony raised his eyebrows at his sister. "Since when did that ever matter? Remember the bit about not being teens?"

Mom came up and rested her arm across Gina's shoulder. "Don't discourage him. Dad and I love Kenna, and your nonna, who probably knows her better than any of the rest of us, is over the moon."

As though Nonna showed that much enthusiasm for anything, ever.

"Where would you guys live?" Gina went on, shrugging off Mom's arm. "That basement suite is awfully small."

"It's not a decision that needs to be made any minute soon. Nonna's doing well now, but she is eighty, and her independence will likely change again at some point. We could make do in the suite, or Kenna has an apartment, or we could rent or buy somewhere. Or we could move right in upstairs with Nonna. It doesn't matter."

"I love you, Auntie Kenna!" came Emma's high, sweet voice from the living room.

The kitchen threesome turned toward the doorway.

"Are you going to marry Unca Tony and have a bee-yoo-tiful wedding like Peetah?"

Tony held his breath, but couldn't help the small grin poking at his cheeks.

"Do you think I should?" asked Kenna.

"Oh, yes. And then I could have a cousin, right? Because Gavin will gets cousins from Peetah."

Oh, boy. Tony started for the living room. Why had he left Kenna alone with the children, anyway? Who knew where kid minds and mouths would go?

"Lots of people don't have babies, you know," Kenna answered evenly. "You might not get cousins."

Tony let out a breath when he caught sight of Kenna smiling down at the little blond munchkin nestled at her side.

"I gots cousins now," Emma continued. "Devon and Adrian and Sam. But they're all boys."

"Yay boys!" Five-year-old Ethan pumped his arm in the air. "And Arie. Don't forget Arie."

"Arie's not our cousin." Emma peered around Kenna at her brother. "He's a... a..."

"Second cousin." Tony crossed the room to kneel in front of Emma then rested one hand on Kenna's knee. "A second cousin is when your moms or dads were cousins first. Your mom and Arie's dad, Marco, are cousins."

Ethan cocked his head to one side. "And you?"

"And me. I'm their cousin, too. I have lots of them, like Marco, which means even if Auntie Kenna and I don't have kids, you guys still have lots of Santoro cousins, as well as the boy cousins from your daddy's brother."

"But I want a girl cousin!" Emma's lower lip protruded as she crossed her little arms.

"Fran and Jasmine and I said that a lot," Gina put in dryly. "We had so many boy cousins it was crazy. And then eventually there were more girls, way younger than us. God gets to decide things like that."

Kenna's fingers clenched Tony's. He took his cue, rocking back and standing, drawing her up with him. He wrapped his arms around her and pulled her close.

"Ew, mushy stuff." Ethan pressed his hands over his eyes.

Tony chuckled at the sight of his nephew's brown eyes peering between pudgy fingers. He gave Kenna a quick kiss. "Wanna go for a walk in the moonlight while Gina puts her kidlets to bed?"

Emma's eyes grew round. "We get to stay at Grandma's house for Christmas? That's the best present ever."

Ethan bounced off the love seat. "There will be better ones tomorrow. Come on, Emma. Bet I can get my jammies on quicker'n you."

"No, me!" She darted after him.

Gina rolled her eyes and followed her children.

A few minutes later, Tony and Kenna had bundled up. He took her mittened hand in his as they wandered down the short lane to the town overlook. Streetlights lit the scene in even grids, and lots of houses were festooned in Christmas lights. Some even had lit-up Santas and nativity scenes. It all brought back a sense of nostalgia. "Galena Landing has grown some since I was a kid."

"Do you miss it?"

He slid his arm around her waist. "In some ways, I guess. When I was a teen, I just wanted to get out. Typical small-town kid, I guess. If a guy admitted he planned to stay, he was obviously a loser. No ambition."

"Why didn't you come back here to start your restaurant?"

Tony shook his head. "Too small." He pointed out a low log structure in the distance. "That's The Sizzling Skillet, where I worked as a dishwasher until I got fired. And over there you see the one-and-only chain drive-through. There are several diners downtown." He shook his head. "Small towns are great for ambience, but not so much for a restaurant like Antonio's."

Kenna rested her head against his. "A nice place to visit."

"Exactly." He gathered her in. "But we didn't come out here to talk about my misspent youth."

"We didn't?" She angled her head and grinned up at him, the moonlight caressing her rosy cheeks.

Tony leaned closer and kissed her nose. "Not even a little bit." He trailed kisses across her eyelids, which fluttered closed at his approach. "Other things are more important." He swept his lips across hers. "Like this." And then he captured her mouth with his and let her know just what he was thinking.

KENNA HAD NEVER EXPERIENCED a Christmas morning like this one. Gina's husband, Chris, awakened Ethan and Emma around seven. Maybe they were too young for an internal alarm clock that screamed *Santa!* in their ears in the wee hours. But though the two eyed the pile of presents under the tree and the overstuffed stockings on the mantle, they seemed patient enough.

Wait a sec. Kenna studied the row of stockings. Eight of them? And a delicately quilted one had her name embroidered on it. No way. Her hand flew up to cover her mouth, and she glanced at Tony.

He leaned closer, his eyes twinkling. "Mom made it for you."

"But... it has my name on it." Like she belonged. Like she was permanent. She managed a shaky breath. "And your parents have some, too? I thought it was only for kids."

"Not in my family." Tony chuckled. "Gina and I didn't want to give up stockings when we got older, so we made a pact with Mom and Dad that each of us would pick up two or three little things to tuck in everyone else's stocking. Late Christmas Eve, we take turns adding our stuff, making sure not to peek inside."

"I didn't know. I would have—"

He kissed her. "This year, you're a guest."

This year? What about in the future? More than anything, she wanted a future with Tony.

His dad brought a tray in from the kitchen. "Hot chocolate for the kids. Coffee for the adults." Matt set the children's mugs on coasters on the coffee table before turning to Kenna. "I think this one is fixed the way you like it."

She couldn't believe the attentiveness. The spoiling, really. She reached for the rustic pottery mug. "Thank you."

Matt sat down and read the Christmas story from the book of Luke. The family sang a couple of carols, and the children's sweet voices carried *Away in a Manger*. Then Matt prayed a blessing over each person in the room. "Father God, thank You for bringing Kenna and Tony together, and I ask that You would guide them in their future. I pray that You would bless Kenna for the great care she's given my mamma. I ask that You would lavish her with Your love. That You would keep her close to You."

He went on to pray for other members of his family, but Kenna's heart was so full it overflowed her eyes. She clenched Tony's hand and knew, no matter what happened, she could never be happier or more loved than she was right here, right now.

EPILOGUE

The upscale lounge was packed with men in tuxedoes and women in gowns seated at small round tables.

Tony had claimed, over and over, that it no longer mattered if Antonio's won an award from the culinary guild but, now that he was here at the annual gala, his heart rate skittered and his hands were clammy.

But Kenna was in her element in a gorgeous pink gown. On a whim — and as a nod to their early days — he'd asked the florist to tuck a few sprigs of lavender in her wrist corsage. It had brought a chuckle and a kiss. Totally worth the effort.

Soon the host began the presentations. Tony's knee jittered as he sat through the best bar, the best coffee spot, the best food truck. But then the woman in the black gown leaned back into the mic. "It's challenging to launch a brand-new upscale restaurant and make a splash within the first year, but Spokane saw some great contenders this year.

Several were highly reviewed and recommended, but the top spot goes to..."

Tony held his breath as she opened the envelope.

"Antonio's on West Main! Chef Santoro, would you accept this award on behalf of your restaurant?"

Polite applause filled the room, but it was Kenna's fingers squeezing his that anchored him. "Go, you," she whispered around a huge smile.

Cameras flashed as he made his way to the podium and accepted the coveted award. He held it up with a big smile then tugged his speech out of his chest pocket. "Thank you, Spokane! Thank you for visiting Antonio's and giving us the chance to wow you with our updated Italian cuisine. My nonna will treasure this award and tell all her friends how much influence she had in my training."

Light laughter filtered through the lounge.

"And she won't be wrong. I'd also like to thank Chef Claire Kenzie of Galena Landing for inspiring a cheeky teenager, my instructors at Seattle Culinary School for teaching me to wield a knife, and my uncle, Chef Leo Ricci, of Italiana in Twin Falls, for teaching me how to run a kitchen."

He paused at the ripple of applause and took a deep breath before meeting Kenna's gaze. She sat with her eyes shining and her mouth parted in a beautiful smile.

"And lastly, I'd like to thank the woman who's come alongside me in the past few months and allowed me to cook for her because, ladies and gentlemen, she needs a chef. You might not know, but there are people who can't heat water without burning it."

She was still smiling. Good. He reached into his pocket and held her gaze.

"She's encouraged my dreams and inspired my creations. Thank you, Makenna Marie Johnson. Will you marry me?"

Tony drew out the small box and angled it as he opened it. Camera flashes compounded, some aimed at him, and some aimed at Kenna. He held his smile and his breath and his pose for a very long moment.

Kenna's eyes widened and her tapered fingers pressed to her chest. She slowly rose to her feet. "Tony!" she gasped as she ran toward him. No small feat with the guests tightly packed. She threw herself in his arms, rocking him backward. "Yes!"

Tony plucked the diamond from its nest and slid it on Kenna's finger. He kissed her lightly — there'd be time for more later — and held their joined hands so the diamond gleamed in the barrage of flashes. "Thank you to the guild for honoring Antonio's, but ladies and gentlemen, this woman right here honors me most of all. Thank you."

He followed Kenna back to their table amid hand slaps and murmured congratulations. He set the award on the table and slid his arm across her shoulders, gathering her as closely as he could in the curved-back chairs. "I love you, sweetheart."

"I never expected this." She fingered the ring then looked at him, eyes shining. "But thank you... and thank God."

"Always and ever." He nuzzled her hair.

It would be impolite to leave before the final awards had been given, wouldn't it? Because he could hardly wait to get his fiancée alone and begin planning for their life together.

DEAR READER...

Thanks for reading *Lavished with Lavender*! I'm so honored that you chose to spend the last few hours with Kenna, Tony, and me. You are appreciated.

I'm an independent author who relies on my readers to help spread the word about stories you enjoy. Would you take a few minutes to let your friends know? Facebook, Twitter, Goodreads... wherever you hang out online.

Also, each honest review at online retailers means a lot to me and helps other readers know if this is a book they might enjoy. I'd sure appreciate your help getting word out.

I welcome contact from readers. At my website, you can contact me via email, read my blog, and find me on social media. You can also sign up for my newsletter to be notified of new releases, contests, special deals, and more! Click here to subscribe. You'll receive *Promise of Peppermint*, the novella that introduces Bridgeview — Rebekah and Wade's story — absolutely free as my thank you gift!

Keep reading for a sneak peek of the next Urban Farm

Fresh Romance book, *Cadence of Cranberries* (Winnie and Charlie's story). Enjoy!

- Valerie Comer

www.valeriecomer.com

http://valeriecomer.com/subscribe

CHAPTER 1

Cadence of Cranberries
An Urban Farm Fresh Romance 10

The usual?"

Winnie Santoro nodded, blinking back sudden moisture in her eyes. "Thank you." When was the last time someone besides her kids had remembered her preferences for ten minutes, let alone an entire week? Since Al, that's when. And her husband been gone for over two years now.

The man in the coffee truck moved with quiet efficiency, prepping her latte and adding an artful flourish of whipped cream on top. He smiled at her as he slipped a sleeve on the paper cup and set it on the ledge.

"Do you remember everyone's orders?" She handed him her payment.

His blue eyes twinkled. "Just the pretty ladies who come alone."

She'd asked for that, but she couldn't fault him for the flirt. He looked to be a bit older than her fifty years, with lightly salted thinning hair. His cranberry red Henley sported the emblem of Redband Roasters, a stylized version of Spokane's signature redband trout.

For once, there was no one behind her waiting for their cup of java at the Kendall Yards Night Market. With frost in the air this October evening, she'd have thought lots of people would need a warmup.

"What do you do with the truck when the markets close in fall?" Not that it was any of her business, but today had been a hard day, and she needed to stay distracted for more than thirty seconds.

"This will be my first winter since I bought the company, but I've got a three-pronged plan." He smiled again, the skin around his eyes crinkling as he did.

His face was made for smiling. "Oh?" Suddenly, Winnie actually wanted to know.

"I'm booked for area festivals through the Christmas season, I've got a place to park the truck near offices downtown weekdays, and I plan to approach more local restaurants about carrying my brand."

"It's terrific coffee. You shouldn't have any trouble finding outlets." She sipped the brew. Probably had a whipped cream mustache, too. She reached for the dispenser only to find the man was already handing her a napkin.

"I should hire you as a spokeswoman."

Winnie chuckled as she dabbed her lip. "Have you approached the owners of Bridgeview Bakery and Bistro?

They might be willing to talk." She pointed across the river in the general direction.

"I haven't. Frankly, I've been too busy learning the ropes of my new business and running the truck over the summer. They're on my list, though."

"Tell them Winnie sent you. Not that I have any influence there."

"Winnie. That's a lovely name." He reached through the opening. "I'm Charlie."

"Pleased to meet you. Officially." She shifted the cup to her left hand and shook his hand. He might not wear the calluses like Al had obtained from years of trimming trees, but Charlie's grip was firm nonetheless. The warmth of it filtered through her. Welcome, but strange.

He looked out over the evening market for a moment, and she turned to do the same, sipping the latte. Canvas gazebos lined both sides of Summit Parkway, but the crowds that had thronged the area even half an hour ago had thinned out as darkness fell.

Winnie was going to miss these Wednesday evening excursions. She told the boys she needed to pick up farm-fresh vegetables, so she made sure to come home with something. A few squash — neither of the boys' favorite — a jar of fiery salsa, maybe some pastured chicken or gourmet cheese or a boule of artisan sourdough. Honestly, she came more for the outing than the shopping.

And for her weekly specialty latte... but if anyone thought to approach the truck, she was blocking their trajectory. No one seemed to be angling this direction, though, and she didn't feel like moving.

"Mr. Winnie doesn't prefer to come to the night market?"

Mr. Winnie? Right, she hadn't offered her surname. Probably because there were so many Santoros in Spokane this man probably knew one of them, or maybe ten. Tonight, she wanted incognito. To be just herself. But his curious gaze was fixed on her wedding rings. She should take them off, but that seemed so final. So traitorous. "He is enjoying dancing in heaven at the feet of Jesus."

"I'm sorry. None of my business."

"It's been over two years." Winnie hesitated. "Today would have been our twenty-seventh wedding anniversary." Which summed up why this had been an uncharacteristically melancholy day. Not that she needed to dump it all on a stranger.

"So... not quite twenty-five."

The man could do math. "We had plans for our silver anniversary. A big party and then a Caribbean cruise. We were going to learn to snorkel." Winnie shook her head. "Sorry for dumping all that. It's been a strange day, but it's not on you."

"Not a problem. Twenty-five years is quite a feat in this day and age." This time it was he who stared off. Then he turned a lopsided smile on Winnie. "My ex and I made it all the way to seventeen."

Ex. So Charlie was divorced, not widowed. *But he's single now.* Winnie shushed her brain, because what did that matter? She might be lonely, but she wasn't looking for a relationship.

Nor did she wish to know the details of Charlie's failed marriage, which meant he was equally as interested in hearing about Al. In other words, she'd overstayed her welcome in front of the Redband Roasters truck.

Winnie lifted the paper cup in salute. "I still have my

shopping to do, so I should get on with it and quit holding up your time. Thanks for the coffee, and have a good evening."

And a nice life, since this was the final market of the season. No point in giving Charlie another thought. She'd never seen him anywhere but at Kendall Yards, so it was unlikely she'd run into him at random around the city.

Unless, of course, she attended the Christmas festivals and sought out his coffee truck.

But a respectable widow of fifty with three teens left in the house, living surrounded by her late husband's extended family, wouldn't do such a thing. She'd keep Al's memory alive every day for their kids and be thankful for the precious years they'd had.

She'd had it good. She knew that. It wasn't fair to expect a second chance.

"Thanks for stopping by, Winnie."

She'd already turned away and taken a few steps, but now she looked back.

Charlie stood illuminated in the truck window, that lopsided smile back on his face. He raised a hand in farewell.

A man who was trying to start something would say something now, but he didn't. He turned to his sink and turned on the faucet.

Just as well.

"Hey, Dad?"

Charlie Jalonen shifted his cellphone to his other hand

and settled into his big comfy chair. "Hey, baby! How are you?"

"Great! I know I told you I couldn't get time off over Thanksgiving, but one of the other nurses in my unit needs the following weekend off for a wedding, so we're swapping shifts."

He barely dared to hope but couldn't help himself. "And...?"

"And Dominic wants me to meet his family." Katri gave a little squeal, and Charlie pictured her bouncing around her small apartment. "Dad, do you think that means what I hope it means?"

Back in the day, a young man would ask his girlfriend's dad for his blessing before proposing. Guess that was kind of old-fashioned now. Charlie could only be thankful one of his daughters had let him back in her life at all after all the venom their mother had spewed. He didn't deserve the lies Julia told, but he *had* been at work too much and therefore a lousy father. Julia was right about that part.

"I don't know, baby. Maybe it depends on what you think it means." He kept his tone light, teasing. She didn't need to know the wound her words scratched open.

"He's amazing, Dad. You're going to love him."

Doubtful any young buck could win over a cynical father like Charlie, but whatever.

"And I think it's pretty cool that you moved to Spokane so the whole meet-the-parents thing can go both ways in one weekend trip."

Charlie dared breathe. His baby girl was really coming home in a couple of weeks. Not that it was home to her, but he could hardly wait to show her around the city. At least if he could pry her away from that boyfriend for an hour or two.

"Has your mother met him?" Why, oh why, had he allowed the question to slip out? At least he'd kept the tone neutral.

"Yes, she has."

Of course. Julia still lived in Seattle. She probably had the young couple over for dinner once a week. He'd missed out on so much over the years. Still was.

"She's thrilled he's a doctor. Well, when he finishes med school next year. Mom figures he'll be able to support a family well."

There were so many things Charlie wanted to say to that. If Julia thought Charlie had worked long, irregular hours at Boeing, she shouldn't be encouraging Katri to marry a doctor, of all things. Money couldn't replace time with his wife and kids. Charlie knew that now. He'd even kind of known it then, but what was a man to do? His career had provided the big house, the two luxury cars in the garage, the upscale vacations, and everything his family could want.

Except a great marriage. Except time with his daughters.

The woman from the night market popped into his mind, not for the first time in the past few weeks. A woman whose husband had passed away and was obviously still grieving two-years-and-a-bit later. She'd once had what Charlie wanted, but hers hadn't lasted, either.

"Dad?"

He blinked. "Pardon me?"

"I asked if you have a spare bedroom for me, but you were so quiet I wasn't sure if the call had dropped."

"I'm here." Just sidetracked. "Yes, I made sure to build in a second bedroom so you or your sister could visit anytime." Not that Evie would be showing up any day soon. She'd swallowed Julia's poison.

"Okay, good. Dominic said I could stay with his sister, but that just seems awkward since we haven't met. Plus, he's going to his cousin's wedding on Saturday. He invited me as his plus one, of course, but I'm not sure about it. Doesn't it seem presumptuous for me to attend a family event? He says he has a million cousins."

"Baby, if you want to go to the wedding, go for it. You'll wow them all. You clean up pretty nice, you know."

Katri chuckled.

"But if you'd rather, you can hang out with me. I'll treasure any time we can spend together."

"Aw, thanks, Dad. I'll let you know what I decide." Her fridge door creaked, and she sighed. "I need to pick up some groceries."

"Do you need money?"

"I've got a job. I got off late and skipped the supermarket on my way home from work. Looks like I shouldn't have."

Charlie already wished he could snatch the words back. He'd always thrown money at every problem. Julia had loved his solution. Until she hadn't.

"Don't forget to eat your veggies."

"Dad!" Katri half-laughed and half-sighed the word.

"Gotcha." If it weren't for Katri's nagging, he'd probably exist on take-out. Turned out he kind of enjoyed cooking, now that he wasn't a burned-out department head in a Fortune 500 company. He should probably have stepped out years ago. Could he have saved his marriage?

Probably not. Nothing satisfied Julia.

"Okay, gotta go. Talk to you soon." Katri popped a kiss into the mic and disconnected.

Charlie set his cell down and wandered over to the large window. Down the hill, through the barren trees, he could make out the Spokane River. A short river, full of obstacles, just like a man's life. Nine of the obstructions were power generators. Was he allowing the obstacles in his life to become something mighty that benefitted those around him? He hoped so. He couldn't undo the past, but his move to Spokane had been a good one. He could start over here. Find a new rhythm.

Once again his mind drifted to the woman. Winnie. The whipped cream clinging to her upper lip. The warmth in her pretty brown eyes. Her delight in the latte she ordered every week. Where was she getting her fix now that the market was closed for the season?

He didn't even know her last name.

Just as well, since she still mourned her husband, and Charlie wasn't looking, either. He was no great catch.

Just ask Julia.

ABOUT VALERIE COMER

Valerie Comer's life on a small farm in western Canada provides the seed for stories of contemporary Christian romance. Like many of her characters, Valerie grows much of her own food and is active in the local foods movement as well as her church. She only hopes her imaginary friends enjoy their happily-ever-afters as much as she does hers, shared with her husband, adult kids, and adorable grand-daughters.

Valerie is a *USA Today* bestselling author and a two-time Word Award winner. She writes engaging characters, strong communities, and deep faith into her green clean romances.

To find out more, visit her website at www.valeriecomer.com, where you can read her blog, explore her many links, and sign up for her email newsletter, where you will find news, giveaways, deals, book recommendations and more. You can also find Valerie blogging with other authors of Christian contemporary romance at Inspy Romance.

www.ingramcontent.com/pod-product-compliance
Lightning Source LLC
Chambersburg PA
CBHW021425200626
46814CB00015B/703